MISSING HER

J. L. WILLOW

Nebula Press, 20 Patrick Henry Pl, Ringoes, N.J. 08551. For any questions about usage, please contact nebulapress@yahoo.com.

Visit the author's website at www.jlwillow.com or contact her at jlwillowbooks@gmail.com.

First Edition.

Paperback ISBN: 978-0-9992526-4-2

Hardback ISBN: 978-0-9992526-2-8

Cover Design by Damzona.

10 9 8 7 6 5 4 3 2 1

To my dearest, closest friends.

Your kindness and compassion will forever live on

in Eliza and Vanessa's undying friendship.

Prologue

THE WOMAN VIOLENTLY threw open the front door. It banged against the wall, the sound echoing through the room.

Ellie giggled, pointing to where the door contacted against the thin plaster. "Look, Mom! There's a dent!"

"Help Brooke with her shoes, Ellie." The woman turned to count the small heads in front of her. Four. "Quickly."

Ellie sauntered over to where her sister stood and guided the toddler to sit on the cool tile floor. Brooke held a worn stuffed bear, which she clutched to her chest with stubby fingers. Ellie looked warily at the cubbyholes built into the wall, debating between the options for footwear. "Should she wear laces or Velcro?"

"Velcro," the woman responded instantly, tossing a pair of light-up sneakers at Ellie with one hand before grabbing two more with the other. "Anthony, Peyton, sit down." The children followed the woman's orders and allowed her to shove on their sneakers. While the dark-haired twins were usually bubbly and lighthearted, something about the hurried tone of the woman's voice disturbed them, so they sat silently, staring up at her with wide eyes as she adjusted their shoes.

Once Brooke's shoes were secured, Ellie helped her up. "Do we need jackets?" Ellie asked, pausing to pull open the creaky closet door.

"No," answered the woman. "We're going in the car."

"But it's cold—"

"You'll be fine."

After attaching the last strap on Anthony's shoe, the woman stood. Anthony and Peyton followed, wobbling slightly on their feet.

"Wait!" Ellie cried suddenly. Before the woman could stop her, she rushed back into the kitchen and emerged a few seconds later holding a brightly colored toy. "I had to get my pinwheel," the child explained, spinning the toy and watching the red and blue swirl.

The woman grabbed Peyton's hand and moved toward the door. "We're going." When the children stared at her, she hissed, *"Move."* Jarred by the sudden sharpness in the woman's tone, the children shuffled quickly to the door, their smiles gone. They had heard that tone before, and they knew it never meant well.

The children stomped outside, unable to match the woman's rushed pace. They shivered in the cold, the crisp air creating clouds of moisture from their breaths.

The woman pulled a set of car keys from her pocket and pointed them at a small blue Civic parked in the driveway. The once-bright color was dulled by a thin sheen of sprayed salt, the small granules finding their way into every crevice from the fender to the corners of the mirrors. The woman smashed her thumb into a button on the keypad. Blipping softly, the car blinked once, signaling that it had been unlocked.

"Mom," Peyton said.

"Okay," the woman clipped. "Get inside. Quickly."

"Mom," Peyton said.

"Watch yourself, Ellie. Don't drag your feet."

"Mom," Peyton said.

"What?" the woman asked abruptly.

"That hurts."

The woman's gaze traveled to where her nails dug into her daughter's arm, pressing waning moons into the little girl's frail skin. "Oh," the woman said. She let go, then picked up Brooke and strapped her into her rear-facing car seat.

Once all the children were safely inside the car, the woman pulled open the driver's side door and sat down. She turned around and quickly did another headcount before starting the engine. After taking a calming breath, she set the gear in reverse and drove the car down the driveway. She didn't check both ways before pulling into the street and speeding off down the suburban road. The engine growled under the hood, sending vibrations through the seats beneath them. While car trips usually resulted in a rowdy cacophony of laughter and happy chatter, the children seemed unwilling to break the tense silence until the woman spoke.

"Okay," she said. "Let's play a game."

The four children cheered, too distracted by the woman's words to catch the tone undercutting them.

"What game?" gasped Ellie. "Is it 'I Spy'?"

"No. It's called 'Duck.'"

"Like 'Duck Duck Goose'?"

"No. This is different. When I tell you to duck, you need

to duck under the seat as quickly as you can and stay quiet and still."

"How do you win?"

"Win?" The woman paused. Her eyes flashed in the afternoon light. "You... you win if you get down the quickest. And you can only sit back up when I say 'Clear.'"

"That's not very fun," Peyton muttered, crossing her arms the way only a four-year-old can.

"It's fun," said the woman, "because you're allowed to take off your seat belts."

There was a collective gasp, followed by a chorus of seat belt clicks. Anthony went limp in his car seat, allowing the car's movements to jostle his small frame. He laughed loudly. The woman jolted at the sound.

"Okay, let's play," she said, forcing a smile. "Duck."

Ellie and the twins threw themselves to the grimy floor. Their small bodies fell onto one another, limbs intertwining. Covering their mouths with their hands, they attempted to stifle their giggles. Brooke remained strapped in, smiling at her siblings' strange actions. She waved the bear in the air, quietly babbling to herself.

After a few seconds, the woman said, "Okay, get up."

"You have to say 'Clear,'" Ellie hissed.

"Clear."

The children sat up, grins etched across their faces. Brooke clapped her hands, unable to comprehend the actions of those around her, but enjoyed the spontaneity of it all the same.

"Did I do good?" Peyton asked.

"Yes, you did." The woman's eyes skimmed the road. She barely blinked.

Ellie stretched her arms up. "I like not wearing a seat belt.

It's bouncy." She pushed herself up from her seat and lowered herself quickly, the foam cushion creating a soft surface to push off. "Bouncy, bouncy, bouncy, bouncy—"

"Duck!"

Again, the children fell to the ground. The scream of a siren cut through the air but quickly faded. The woman's breathing became rapid for a moment before falling back to its normal rhythm. "Clear," she said.

"Was that the police?" Ellie gazed out the rear window, her palms pressed against the glass.

The woman's eyes flicked to the back seat. "Stay away from the windows!" Ellie didn't miss the harshness of the woman's voice, and she jerked away from the glass.

"That's another rule," the woman said after a moment of silence, once again calm. "You have to stay away from the windows."

"Why were the police there?" Peyton asked.

"Something happened."

"Like what?"

"Maybe someone killed a bank."

Ellie laughed. "Killed a bank? How do you kill a bank?"

"I mean robbed a bank. Or killed a..." The woman trailed off, her ears catching the shrill cry of another police car. "Duck!"

The children fell to the floor once more. The woman licked her lips, her gaze flicking to the duffel bag in the passenger seat. She turned on the radio. The sharp hiss of static filled the air. She changed the channel, turned up the volume. It was several seconds, though it seemed like hours to the children, before she said, "Clear."

Ellie had been thinking. "Are we hiding from something? Is that why we have to duck?"

"No," the woman responded quickly. "It's just part of the game. The person running the game gets to decide when everyone ducks."

"Oh! Can I run the game next?"

"Maybe." Glancing at the rearview mirror, the woman frowned at a black car with tinted windows. She put on her turn signal and switched lanes, trying to put a few feet of space between them. The car increased speed just enough to maintain the distance.

Just as the woman started to step on the gas again, a row of lights rose onto the top of the black car. Blue and red flashed. "Shit."

"Mommy," Ellie whispered, hearing the panic lacing the woman's voice. "That's a bad word."

The woman ignored the girl, twisting the steering wheel to change lanes. Her green eyes remained firmly glued to the road ahead of her.

"Mommy?" Anthony whispered. "What's wrong?"

Her gaze flicking to the rearview mirror, the woman growled, "They won't take you away from me." She clutched the steering wheel with a white-knuckle grip. "I won't let them."

"Mommy, what—" Ellie's tearful reply was cut off by the loud shriek of a police siren. It came from directly behind them. Brooke was startled by the sudden noise and started to cry.

"Shut up!" The gas pedal was pressed to the floor, speeding up the outside world until it became a blur of color behind the windows. The police lights reflected inside the car, and the children shielded their eyes against the bright colors. The woman glanced at the car behind them again, then back to the road. It took her a second to comprehend the second cop car stopped several hundred feet in front of them, laying something down onto the road, a metal strip with spikes aiming toward the sky. *"Duck!"* The woman slammed on the brakes, and the children screamed with the tires. But the car skidded forward, over the strip. There were several sharp bangs, like gunshots, before the car began to swerve.

"I can't control it!" the woman screamed, straining against the steering wheel to get the car between the lines of the road. She twisted it all the way to one side, then flipped it to the other.

It all happened at once.

The car spun wildly on the road, riding over a rumble strip and careening into the middle barrier. The force of the impact shoved it back across the road, burning black marks into the asphalt before it came to a stop over the yellow double line.

A police car pulled up alongside the demolished vehicle, and an officer emerged, gun drawn. He paused, listening for movement behind the shattered windows.

The silence was broken only by Brooke's screams.

I

A SUDDEN GUST of wind tore the paper from my grasp. It danced and spun in the air, twirling as it rocketed toward the sky. Pushing a lock of black hair behind my ear, I followed it with my eyes until it dashed behind a bush and out of sight. I glanced down at the other copies clutched between my fingers, wrinkled from the pressure needed to keep them in place. From each of the pages, two bright eyes and a wide smile met my stare. I had to force my gaze away from them. It was worse to see her actual face than to just hear her name.

Eliza Barrows. One of the most beloved girls in Mount Sterling. At least she used to be. It only took one night and one mistake for everything to change.

Reaching into the satchel crossing over one shoulder, I pulled out a stapler. Pressing another "Missing Person" flyer over the vacant area on the wooden utility pole, I put a staple in each of the four corners. Even in grainy black and white, she still looked just as I remembered her. And aside from grainy cell phone photos, that's the only thing I could base her looks on now—memory.

Eliza and I had one of those friendships you see in the movies but never actually think could happen in real life. For all of second grade, we sat across each other at one of those large round tables with barely enough legroom. Some best friends have that immediate connection, but it took us a little longer to find each other. We were nice to each other but not super close until I failed my spelling test one day.

I, seven years old, was sitting at recess, gripping the paper in both hands as tears streamed down my face. I vividly remember my eyes staring at the big red "F" at the top corner of the page and the words "FIX AND RETURN TO ME" written right at the bottom.

When I heard someone approaching, I crumpled up the paper and wiped at my face with my sleeve before shoving it into my bag. "What?" I sniffed at Eliza.

She was holding a paper in her hands too. She spun it around so I could see the red marks. "Did you fail too?" she asked.

My eyes flicked from her to the paper, then sighed. "Yeah. My mom's gonna be so mad."

Eliza walked to sit beside me. "I don't think so," she replied. "The test was way too hard. Who needs to know how to spell 'Wednesday,' anyway?"

"I know!" I pulled the test out of my bag, pointing at the second answer. "She told us to sound it out, so I did! W-E-N-Z-D-A-Y. How was I supposed to know the 'Z' was an 'S'?"

"And there's an extra 'D' in the middle! For no reason!"

We talked and laughed together for the rest of recess, bonding over our shared hatred of the English language. And from that moment, we were inseparable. We went everywhere together, did everything together. Whether it was auditioning for the school production of *Cinderella* or shopping at the mall, it was always the two of us. You would've thought we would be sick of each other by the time high school rolled around. Even all those years later, though, I couldn't imagine life without Eliza.

But now I didn't have to imagine. I had lived it every day for nearly five months. I forced myself out my memories when I heard someone approach from behind me.

"Isn't that kind of pointless now?"

I crinkled my nose at the familiar voice, stopping in my tracks. Hoping he would heed the warning in my gaze, I turned to face Dwight. "What did you say?"

He leaned against the CVS on my right, chewing noisily on a stick of gum. His lanky arms were crossed in front of him as he sagged his weight into the doorframe. Rather than looking cool and casual as he surely expected himself to appear, he gave off an air of idiotic flamboyance.

"The flyer thing," he answered, snapping the gum between his back teeth. "According to the laws of probability, they're not going to find her."

"Shut up, Dwight."

Squinting his dark eyes at me, he shrugged in an *I'm-just-telling-it-like-it-is* sort of way. "After forty-eight hours, the chances of finding a missing person go down nearly 70 percent. Besides, everyone in this area knows what she looks like, so it's not like putting up a flyer will magically make someone recognize her."

I pulled my cell phone and earbuds out of my coat pocket, stuffed one bud into each ear, and turned up the collar of my coat: the universal gesture for "go away." "I *really* don't need your smart-assery right now."

Dwight chuckled, refusing to back down even as I turned away. "I'm not being a smart-ass. I mean, I know I can be sometimes. Well, most of the time. But there's a difference between being a smart-ass and being realistic."

I whipped around to face him. He nearly didn't stop walking in time, and his face stopped inches from my own. "Yeah, there's a difference between the two, and right now, you're just being a smart-ass. So why don't you go home and play your Xbox and stay out of what you don't know shit about?"

Realizing he had pushed too far, Dwight held my gaze for a moment longer before moving away. I could've sworn he muttered something that rhymed with "itch," but I let it go. When deciding between getting into an argument with that kid and just walking away, I'd choose the latter any day.

My feet pounded the well-traversed path, moving mechanically with my mind on autopilot. It took a moment, but I slowly became acclimated to the song my phone had randomly shuffled. AC/DC. My steps automatically fell in time with the beat. I allowed my head to bob with the throbbing guitar, the heartbeat of the music setting the pace for my thoughts.

One step at a time. Don't look back.

At this point, hanging the "Missing Person" posters was just an empty routine. I checked each of the spots I had been assigned, making sure the copy hadn't been taken down or blown away. It wasn't groundbreaking work, but it helped me convince myself that I was making some sort of headway to find my friend. The police had already interviewed everyone from the party—the last place Eliza had been seen—and found nothing. No suspects, no evidence, not a single witness. It was as if she vanished without a trace. Now, any hope we had of picking up a trail on the case was rapidly diminishing. People kept saying not to give up, that we'd find her eventually. I promised myself I wouldn't stop, but I'd be lying if I said it wasn't getting harder and harder to keep moving as each day passed.

My eyes caught an empty spot on the billboard outside the county library. Reaching for another flyer, I hissed as I felt the sharp sting of a paper cut. The blood blossomed from the thin laceration on the tip of my pointer finger. I lightly pressed it to my lips, and a hint of copper touched my tongue. Still nursing the one hand, I cautiously withdrew a paper with the other and stapled it into place.

I'm not giving up.

By the time I had finished, the sky was growing dark. The sun had fallen west, casting an orange-tinged glow across the sidewalk. I reached down to latch the satchel shut and turned back toward the center of town. Time to head back.

During my return journey, I passed a few people I knew. At least they acted like they knew me. I never learned the trick of remembering faces. If they said anything, it was blocked out by the pulsating classic rock in my ears. Luckily, I wasn't that far from the house, so I didn't have to politely smile and half-wave too many times.

Turning off the sidewalk, I started toward the small suburban house. It had a brick exterior with small windows and a dark shingled roof. Even though on the outside it looked like every other house in the cramped neighborhood, this one seemed to exude an air of mystery and fear. Although that was usually enough to turn people away, it didn't slow me down. I stomped up the weather-worn steps, scraping my feet into the two trenches worn into the welcome mat. As I prepared to knock, I paused, staring at my reflection in the windowpane set into the center of the door.

The bags under my dark brown eyes had become more pronounced. If I didn't know better, I would've thought that they were smears of mascara. But I did know better, and I knew that makeup remover wouldn't do any good. I had always been pale-skinned, and the whiteness was stark contrast to the darkness of my other features. After a moment, I looked away. The more I looked at myself, the less I saw of me and the more I saw of what I had become.

When I rapped my knuckles three times against the stained wood of the door, they came away red. The recent rainfall must have dampened the wood and loosened the paint.

The door flew open two seconds later, revealing the hopeful, tired face of Mrs. Barrows. As soon as she recognized me, her face fell. "Oh hi, Vanessa," she said softly, voice barely carrying to my ear.

"Hi, Mrs. Barrows."

Her brown eyes swept the area behind me, searching for someone I knew she wouldn't find, before opening the door wider and ushering me inside. "How many times do I have to tell you you don't need to knock? Just come inside, you're practically family."

"Okay." I stepped inside the dimly lit room and slipped off my tennis shoes. Every week we had the same exchange of empty words, empty actions, all for the same hopeful cause that ultimately led to harrowed disappointment.

Mrs. Barrows stepped timidly inside, knowing without looking behind her that I was following. "How did it go today?" she asked, pausing to pull out a chair for me at the kitchen table before doing the same for herself.

I nodded my thanks and sat down. "No issues. I only needed to replace a few posters."

Mrs. Barrows moved to sit across me. She moved slowly, without the spring that had always rebounded her step. It hadn't been present for weeks. "Vanessa." Reaching across the table, she took both my hands and wrapped them in her own. "It's been five months."

"Yes, I know," I replied quickly, tightening my grip on hers to emphasize my words. "And I feel like we're getting closer. We just got that tip recently about seeing her in the city, and with the posters…" My words faded to silence when I saw the look on Mrs. Barrows' face. "The tip?"

She shook her head, the pain written into her features. "It was a fake."

I absorbed the news quickly, heart sinking a bit. "Okay," I continued after a moment's pause, "but we're still making progress. We'll get there. We'll find her."

"Yes, we will." Mrs. Barrows cast her eyes down, refusing to meet mine. "But, Vanessa, I think… I think my husband and I can keep up the search on our own."

I shook my head. "I really don't mind. I'm happy to help."

"We've been so grateful for your help." She took a breath, holding it for as long as she could before the rest of the sentence came rushing out. "But it's time for you to move on."

The words she spoke stole my own. It took a moment to regain my breath, and when I did, the air that filled my lungs was heavy. "What?"

"Don't think we're giving up," Mrs. Barrows said quickly, lifting her gaze to meet mine. She weighed her next words carefully. "We're not giving up. But you need to start focusing on other things. You have college coming up and applications—"

"That can wait," I responded firmly. "Eliza is more important."

"We want you to have a life, Vanessa. I know she was your best friend, and you've given so much time to helping the search—"

Was. "No. She is *still* my best friend. And I'm not stopping until she's found."

"Vanessa." Mrs. Barrows tone had shifted. It was cold now, hard. Even though her tone was firm, her eyes remained fixed to the floor. "You need to focus on your future. Let us continue looking for Eliza. If anything new comes along, we'll let you know. But for now, study for school, join some clubs. Try to live a normal life."

I opened my mouth, but nothing came out. How could I just go back to a normal life? Like my best friend of eleven years hadn't vanished off the face of the earth? The answer was simple: I couldn't.

"Please," I begged, forcing the words past the tightness in my chest. "I need to do *something.*"

Mrs. Barrows finally met my gaze, our shared anguish binding us together. "I know. And Eliza would've wanted you to get into a good college and have a happy life—"

I shot up, and my chair squealed against the tile floor. "Don't tell me what Eliza *would've wanted.* Eliza is alive. When we find her, we'll ask her what she wants."

Mrs. Barrows stared at me. Her eyes were empty. They weren't cold or angry. They were drained. "Vanessa," she murmured, pressing her fingers to her temples. "Don't make this harder than it needs to be. I'm just trying to do the right thing. For everyone." Her eyes finally lifted to meet my own as her hands dropped to the table. "We'll keep in touch. I promise to let you know if anything comes up, anything at all."

I stared at her for a long moment. With one hand, I pulled the satchel off my shoulder, ignoring how the rough material chafed my neck, and dropped it on the table. A few flyers escaped, fluttering to the floor. I couldn't help but glance down at them, catching a glimpse of straight blond hair and bright eyes. When I pulled my gaze back to Mrs. Barrows, I read her pain, her fear, her doubt. But I also saw her small relief that she was removing someone from the hell she was living.

I wasn't angry with her. I was angry with the community, with the police who couldn't find her. A girl doesn't just go to a party and disappear. Something happened that night. Why couldn't anyone figure out what? I had nothing more to say, so I left without another word.

The walk home was long, made longer by the fact that it had started to rain. With nothing to do but listen to the pounding heartbeat in my ears, I pulled out my earbuds again and flipped to my most recent playlist. After a few seconds, a quiet, acoustic strumming met my ears, which I instantly identified as Pink Floyd. I relied on the singer and pensive guitar to express what I couldn't.

In those last five months, I'd discovered that helplessness is the most painful emotion a human can experience. With anger or sadness or fear, there's usually something the emotion is stemming from that can be resolved or at the very least lessened. With helplessness, there's nothing that can be done. There's nothing anyone can do.

Eliza was out there somewhere. And there was nothing I could do about it.

The thought fell over me, its weight caving my shoulders downward. Even music, the thing that usually gave me refuge, couldn't help me this time. And that's when the singer voiced the title of the song.

"Wish You Were Here."

II

I SLUNK INTO my bedroom, tossing my jacket across the unmade bed. Spinning to face the door, I allowed gravity to pull me downward and I fell onto the plush mattress. The stained ceiling that faced me was depressing, an off shade of white speckled with water damage. Searching for a better view, I pulled out my phone and texted the only person whose advice I trusted as much as Eliza's.

Jeremy was technically my cousin, but he felt more like a brother who just happened to live in Alabama. The country air seemed to give him a better perspective on life, and he always knew just what to say, no matter the circumstance.

Vanessa: hey

It didn't take long before I heard the text tone signaling his response.

Jeremy: hey wassup

Jeremy: glad u found ur phone

I furrowed my brow at his words, confused.

Vanessa: wat r u talking about

Jeremy: ur phone. u told me u lost it.

Vanessa: no i didnt

There was a pause before he texted back.

Jeremy: oh okay. guess i got confused with someone else

Vanessa: no problem

Jeremy: so... how r u doing

Vanessa: :(

Jeremy: why r u :(

Vanessa: mrs barrows told me to stop helping out with the posters for eliza

Jeremy: ???

Jeremy: y??

Vanessa: she wants me to focus on school and stuff

Vanessa: which is bs

Jeremy: i mean, i'm sure she's just trying to do the right thing

I rolled my eyes, stabbing at the keys with both thumbs.

Vanessa: I SWEAR if i have to hear the words "right thing" one more time

Vanessa: the "right thing" to do is to find eliza. school can wait.

Jeremy: okay okay chill just trying to help

I forced myself to check my anger. He understood the situation and how delicate it all was. I already knew that nothing he could say would lessen my frustration. I just needed someone to vent to, someone who could begin to understand what I was going through.

Vanessa: i know, im sry. i just dont know what to do anymore

A few minutes passed before I received a reply, making me think he was preparing one of his classic life lessons. When I read what he had typed, I wasn't disappointed.

Jeremy: i dont think you should just give up and stop trying. thats not right. but you do need to start preparing for what comes next. we cant stay in the past forever. it may feel like surrender, but its not. pray that Eliza is safe and that she will be found. let God do his work.

I gave a rough laugh as I typed.

Vanessa: god hasnt done jackshit for me

Jeremy: well have you ever tried talking to Him?

Jeremy: like, really talking to Him?

Before I could try to draft a response, I heard a knock on my bedroom door.

"Come in," I said, pulling my physics textbook to me and flipping it open. The door slowly swung open, revealing the timid smile of my dad.

"Hey, sweetie," he said softly, taking a step into the room. "How are you?"

"Good." I lifted the book so he could see the cover. "Just studying."

"Oh physics!" Chuckling, he walked to stand beside me and look over my shoulder. "When I was your age, I was great in that class. Force equals acceleration times mass, all that good stuff."

I nodded, pursing my lips. We were actually way ahead, having just finished our circuits unit, but forces was the first page I flipped open to. "Yeah, it's pretty cool."

My dad nodded again, seemingly lost in thought. Then he stepped back toward the door. "Good talk," he said enthusiastically, then paused. "Oh, honey, your mother wanted to ask if you were coming down for dinner."

I shook my head. "No, I grabbed something to eat on the way home from school." I hadn't actually, but I really wasn't hungry. The conversation with Mrs. Barrows had stolen my appetite.

"Okay! Well, I'll see you later then." I returned the smile my dad gave me, then watched as he closed the door. I didn't mean to be snippy. I just couldn't handle human interaction at the moment.

Pulling my phone back out, I reread my most recent text from Jeremy. He was always trying to push the faith angle, even though he knew I never believed in all that. I heaved a sigh and glanced at the clock. It was nearly eight. I needed to make at least a little headway in my homework before I surrendered to sleep's numbing embrace. After pulling out some spare sheets of notebook paper, I turned to the correct page in my physics textbook and began.

By eleven thirty, my mind was drenched with concepts of currents and magnetic fields. I rubbed my eyes and squinted at the page. The words swam in front of me, forcing me to accept the fact that I wouldn't get any more work done tonight.

Closing the textbook, I placed it on the floor beside my bed and switched off the lamp on my bedside table. Then I shut my eyes and allowed the darkness to surround me. Jeremy's words resurfaced in my mind's eye. Did I have any other options at the moment? I considered the option pretty useless to say the least, but I decided to try it. What was the worst that could happen? "Nothing" was the worst that could happen, and that had already been happening for months.

"All right, here goes nothing," I whispered to the quiet night air. Then I stilled my mind and tried to focus.

Are you there, God? Hey, isn't that some fifth-grade summer reading book or something? The main girl was Maggie or Meghan or something…

Anyway, I gotta focus. Sorry, it's been so long since You've heard from me. Up until five months ago, everything was going well, but You know that, don't You? Wait, what's the point of this anyway if You can read minds? Don't You know what I'm about to say? Whatever, I don't even want to go down that road right now.

Here's the thing. My friend Eliza… she's gone. They don't know where she is or what happened to her. I need to find her. I don't know what I'm going to do without her.

I paused, trying to swallow the lump forming in my throat. Why was this so hard?

You know I only bother You when it's really important. Well, this is really important. It's the end of the line for me. I have nothing else to do, nowhere else to go. I know that every day that passes decreases the chance that we'll find her. So if You can do anything, or if you have some last trick You'd like to use, this is it—that is, if You're actually listening.

I lay there, waiting for proof that my silent message had reached *someone*. Anyone. But there was nothing. No chorus of angels, no blinding flash of light. Only silence.

Opening my eyes, I stared at the darkness and released the breath I had been holding deep within my chest.

"Are You even listening?" I whispered.

III

I MUST HAVE fallen asleep at some point. When I opened my eyes, I could sense that time had passed. Something felt slightly off, which I chalked up to morning grogginess. So I rolled over and waited for my mind to clear. Once I was ready to process the morning, I pulled my legs over the side of the bed and stood.

Something was definitely different. It was subtle but noticeable. I looked down and noticed I had socks on. I never wore socks to bed. Had I put a pair on last night? Maybe, but I didn't remember it. Shifting my weight from foot to foot, I realized the ground was slightly further away than it should've been. I looked up.

This wasn't my room.

That wasn't my bed or my closet or my door. Turning around, I realized I knew this bedroom. It was Eliza's. But what was I doing in Eliza's bedroom? I automatically glanced to the wall socket for a cell phone, and there it was, in her black and white marbled case. I pressed the home button, and the screen flashed to life, revealing the time as 5:43 a.m. My eyes flicked to the date. I blinked, rubbed my eyes, and read it again.

November 16. But that was the day before…

I spun around, gaze skimming over everything in the room. There was no one here. Stumbling to the door, I turned into the next room I saw, a small bathroom. I flicked on the light, and the bulb sputtered to life. My pupils burned against the sudden white, but once they adjusted, the breath was torn from my lungs.

There she was. Eliza. Looking just as surprised as I was.

"Eliza!" The word ripped itself from my throat. Again, I felt that dissonance of what should be and what was. The voice that spoke wasn't mine. Without thinking, I put a hand to my throat. I looked up and saw Eliza do the same. Why hadn't she said anything? I squinted at the mirror, confused.

The mirror. That wasn't Eliza, that was her reflection. Then who was I looking at?

I moved my hand up to rest on my cheek. My best friend did the same. That's when it clicked.

"Wait," I breathed, the words barely making it past my lips. "*I'm* Eliza?"

PART ONE

Eliza

I

I RAN ONE hand over her cheek (*my* cheek) and through her hair (*my* hair). Was this a dream? It felt so real. As I looked into Eliza's eyes, the confused, hot tear that rolled down one cheek definitely didn't feel like a dream.

My world spun around me as I stepped away from the mirror and struggled to process my surroundings. This was an exact replica of her bathroom, down to the Lush shower jelly and electronic toothbrush. There was no way I could recall all those details on a whim, let alone in a dream.

I backed up slowly, carefully placing one foot behind the other, until my calf hit the side of the tub. I lowered myself to sit on the edge and rested my head in my hands. My lungs were burning from my erratic breathing, so I focused on slowing it down to take in deep, calming breaths.

This was a dream. It had to be. Just a twisted, hyper-realistic dream. That was the only explanation that made even a lick of sense.

As I struggled to wrap my mind around that thought, the

door flew open. I stifled a scream and barely stopped myself from falling backward into the tub.

"Eliza!" exclaimed a familiar, breathy voice. "What are you doing awake?" I looked up, right into the eyes of Mrs. Barrows. Her expression was concerned, but there was a brightness in her eyes I hadn't seen in a long time. Not since… since before Eliza went missing.

"Mrs.—" I caught myself, paused. I wasn't Vanessa anymore. I was Eliza. And if this was a dream, then I needed to go along with it. Play the part. So how would Eliza respond in this scenario? Taking a breath, I forced myself to say, "Mom, I just got up a little early. Bad dream."

"Are you okay?"

Glancing around the room, I replied, "Yeah, I think so."

"All right." Mrs. Barrows gestured toward the staircase across from Eliza's bedroom, heading down to the main floor. "Well, I guess since you got yourself up, all I need to do now is make your lunch. I'll be downstairs."

A meek "okay" was all I could muster in response. I didn't stand right away, fearing my legs wouldn't be able to hold my weight. It was only after she left that I used the towel rack attached to the side wall to shakily lift myself to my feet. Then I turned back to the mirror.

Eliza. I took in every feature of her face: the color of her eyes, the shine of her hair. I soaked it in as if I would never see it again—deep down, I knew there was a chance I wouldn't. Once I woke up and this disappeared, I would be back to where I started: as Vanessa, missing her.

I blinked the moisture from my eyes and narrowed my gaze. If this *was* a dream, then I would wake up eventually. But I had no idea when that would happen. Pinching the top of my hand, I quickly realized that it wouldn't be as easy to wake up from a dream as they made it out to be in the movies. At the moment, there wasn't much else to do except go along with it. And that meant getting ready for school.

Even in the dream state, Eliza was the perfect and prepared girl I remembered her to be. She had laid out her outfit the night before, from slip-on sneakers to matching earrings, everything. All I had to do was find a pair of shoes. It felt weird using her toiletries, but if this dream-Eliza was anything like the real one, I knew she wouldn't miss brushing her teeth. After I put a final swipe of strawberry-scented gloss on my lips, I glanced at the mirror again. I was Eliza—hazel eyes, blond hair, and all. Even as I looked in the reflection, staring at my new physique, I still *felt* like Vanessa. When I reached up to twirl my hair, my brain told me I should've felt frizzy waves instead of naturally straight locks. It was a strange sensation, feeling like one thing when you knew you looked like another. I turned away, a strange sense of vertigo washing over me.

I made my way downstairs without incident. Although my newly acquired height was a little disorienting, it wasn't too noticeable and my equilibrium soon adjusted. By the time I made it to the kitchen, I was walking nearly identical to my normal pace. Mrs. Barrows was cooking something on the electric stove, and I smelled the unmistakable scent of scrambled eggs. The first hints of sunlight were peeking through the window, casting a band of light into my eyes. Hearing my approach, she turned around and smiled.

"Hi, honey. Feeling a little better?"

I nodded, sitting down at the circular table set in the center of the room. "Yeah, thanks."

Mrs. Barrows smiled at me before turning back to the pan. "I'm glad. You looked really pale when I first saw you."

I'm not surprised, all things considered, I thought but didn't say anything. My eyes quickly caught the jug of orange juice on the table, so I picked it up and poured myself a glass. A few seconds later, Mrs. Barrows placed a heaping plate of scrambled eggs on the table before me.

"Enjoy!" she bubbled, stepping away to crack another egg over the side of the pan.

I paused, opening my mouth to say that I wasn't hungry. As I stared at the plate, though, I felt my stomach growl. Suddenly, those eggs looked more than appetizing. Normally, I don't eat breakfast. I'm just not hungry that early in the morning. I'd never understood how Eliza was able to eat before 9:00 a.m.

Well, I thought as I listened to my stomach growl. *Now I understand.* I picked up a fork and dove into the plate. It was heavenly—hot, fresh, and lightly salted. One of the things Eliza and I did have in common was a love of strong coffee, so I was more than happy when Mrs. Barrows placed a steaming cup in front of me. A strong sense of deja vu washed over me as I remembered the many post-slumber party mornings Eliza and I had shared just like this one. Mrs. Barrows only knew how to cook one thing—scrambled eggs—and she made it every time I stayed the night.

For a single moment, I absorbed the scene in front of me. I could almost imagine it was real. Like I was actually spending time with Mrs. Barrows while Eliza was getting ready. Like at any moment, my best friend would come bounding through the door, a wide smile stretched across her face.

But no. This wasn't real life. At least, it wasn't *my* life. This was Eliza's. This was a dream. And I didn't want this real/fake memory of my friend. I wanted the *true* Eliza, alive and well.

"Something wrong with the eggs?"

I shook my head, partially in response to the question and partially in an attempt to refocus. Forcing my lips into something that resembled a smile, I answered, "Nope. I should probably head to the bus."

Mrs. Barrows narrowed her eyes at me slightly, but my grin must have been convincing enough because she nodded. "Okay. Have a great day, sweetie." She walked toward me as I stood. Before I could protest, she pulled me into an embrace. I felt her kiss the top of my head, soft and quick. Keeping both hands on my shoulders, she stepped back to look me up and down. "Wow, I think you grew a bit."

"Yeah," I muttered, blood rushing to my cheeks. "Sorry, I-I gotta go."

After one last long look, Mrs. Barrows let her hands drop to her sides. "Okay, Eliza. Have a great day!"

I nodded and backed away, mind reeling. School. I had to go to school. But as the thought sank in, I froze. I didn't know where Eliza's backpack was. I glanced around, searching for some sort of clue. That's when I had this intuition, this inexplicable feeling that it was in the side closet. I couldn't explain how, but I just *knew* it was there. Moving on pure instinct, I opened the closet. And there it was, lying on the floor. I slowly picked up the dark purple bag trimmed with white and slung it over one shoulder. *Weird*, I thought, but didn't think much more of it. It wasn't like that was the weirdest thing that had happened to me that morning.

After waving once more to Mrs. Barrows, I headed to the door and breathed a sigh of relief when it closed behind me.

I took a moment to gather my thoughts before starting down the driveway. Right on time, the yellow school bus turned the corner and rolled down the street toward me. It pulled to a stop in front of Eliza's driveway, and without stopping to think, I stepped on.

Again, I felt that panic as my eyes swept across the seats. Where did Eliza usually sit? It was high school law that everyone had assigned seats, and I couldn't mess with that system. But again, I felt that instinct: *third row on the left.* I collapsed into the empty three-seater. When the bus started moving again, I rested my head against the window as I tried to catch my breath.

Even though I was in control, it seemed like there was still a little bit of Eliza in my mind, the muscle memory learned through months of habit. Things that Eliza did every day seemed to be ingrained in her brain, and her body moved through the motions without hesitation. So even though I was in control, Eliza's body still knew how to react in certain situations. I made a mental note but didn't dwell on the thought for too long.

With every pothole and bump the bus rolled over, I expected myself to jostle awake and find myself wrapped in familiar blankets. But as the minutes ticked on, it seemed I wasn't "waking up" anytime soon. If this was a dream, it was a weird-ass dream. Even my most twisted imagination couldn't concoct something like this.

If I wasn't asleep while all this was taking place, then there had to be a reason all this was happening. I closed my eyes, trying to think. It didn't take long for me to recall the desperate prayer I had sent up the night before. Some weird coincidence, maybe? Or maybe not. I rolled my eyes up to stare at the studded ceiling of the bus.

"If this is Your doing," I mouthed, "then You are totally messed up."

After yet again receiving no response, I pulled out Eliza's phone and rummaged through her backpack for a few seconds before victoriously retrieving a pair of earbuds. I plugged them into my ears and opened Eliza's phone. I didn't need the help of her subconscious to unlock her phone. Ever since we got matching phone cases in fifth grade, we've known each other's passwords. I scrolled through her playlists, cringing at all the pop hits. At any point in time, someone could take a playlist on her phone, slap on the title of "Top Hits," and make the no. 1 playlist for the year. Eliza liked what everyone else liked, and that was that. Although her lack of original thinking regarding music bugged me, it didn't do me any harm, so I rarely brought it up. But now, when all I wanted was some of my own music to ground me in reality, I was slowly going insane.

The minutes of searching paid off when I found the one pre-2000 song on her phone. It wasn't one of my favorites, a little too overplayed, but "Eye of the Tiger" was leaps and bounds ahead of the other crap she had. I closed my eyes, letting the familiar chords occupy my mind for as long as it lasted.

Luckily, I didn't have to bother searching for another song because just as the last chord was struck, the bus pulled to a stop in front of the high school. I stepped off and quickly became swept up in the mob of students. Even without her instincts, I knew where Eliza's locker was, and I immediately set off toward it.

That's when I felt one hand wrap around my waist and another clench itself over my mouth.

II

I OPENED MY mouth to scream, but the sound was reduced to a muffled cry. My heart pounded against my chest as I struggled in the viselike grip. The hands moved to my shoulders, then spun me around, and I got the first look at my perpetrator.

"Gotcha!" Trevor's deep laugh met my ears, and at last, my pulse began to slow.

Trevor. Eliza's boyfriend of seven months. To be honest, I had forgotten he existed.

"Oh yeah." I tried to force out a laugh. "You sure got me good." If I was going to pass myself off for Eliza, I really needed to stop being so on edge. She was cool as a cucumber, quick to make a joke. I was… not.

Trevor draped an arm over my shoulder, steering me back in the direction I had originally been walking. "How ya doin', babe?"

I tried not to squirm in the unwanted affection. I had always been a little jealous of how Trevor and Eliza were head over heels for each other, but I was not envious of this ooey-gooey crap. "Fine, I guess." I shrugged and somehow thought to add, "I didn't get a chance to do my calc homework, so I'm kinda screwed on that front."

"Well, that class is a joke anyway."

We exchanged a few more friendly remarks, and each time I tried to respond like I thought Eliza would. It was easier than I thought it would be. Maybe I was getting more used to acting like her. Or maybe there was more of her left in this dream-thing than I first thought.

Once we reached my locker, I put my hand up to the combination lock. "Well," I remarked, "I guess I better—"

Trevor cut me off with a kiss. Inside, I jumped about ten feet, but Eliza didn't. She was used to this endearment. It felt wrong, experiencing such an intimate thing that shouldn't have been mine to share. When we broke apart, I forced a smile onto my face and tried to look like I wasn't on the verge of a mental breakdown. Trevor kept his arms draped around my neck and stared deep into my—I mean, Eliza's eyes.

"Are you going to that party tomorrow night?" he asked breathlessly.

"What party?" The confusion was shared between Eliza and me. This was new information to the both of us.

"At Emma's place." He glanced to our left and right before leaning in to add softly, "There's gonna be booze."

My whole body jolted when his words snapped into clarity. *The party*. That was the last place Eliza had been seen alive. If I stayed in Eliza's mind until tomorrow, then I would have to relive the party where she went missing. I had no idea what happened to her that caused her to disappear. The worst options flew into my mind, and I couldn't suppress the shiver that raced down my spine. I didn't know if I could bare to witness whatever happened that night. It might be too much for me.

Then again, who was to say that this reliving of the past was set in stone? What if she didn't *have* to go to the party tomorrow? I was in control, meaning I had some control over what happened. What if I could stop her going to the party?

What if I could save her?

If I saved her now and this really was just a dream, then it would have no impact on reality. But at least it would mean I wouldn't have to watch whatever went down that night that resulted in the disappearance of my friend.

"Um..." I shook my head, trying reorder my thoughts. If this half-baked idea of mine was going to work, there was no way Eliza could go to that party. "I'm not sure... I might have homework—"

"Awh, c'mon, babe." Trevor shifted his hands so they gripped my upper arms. His hold was slightly too tight to be casual. I moved my head to look at them, then back up to his face. "You gotta go," he insisted with a lopsided grin. "For me."

I swallowed. It didn't sound like he was asking. I had never seen him talk to Eliza like this before. Maybe I caught him on a bad day or something.

"I'll think about it," I relented, desperate to end the conversation. I would give him a better excuse later, once I thought of something. At the moment, I just needed to get out of there.

Using one finger to tip my chin up toward his, he whispered, "That's my girl." A movement off to his left caught his attention, and he turned to look. When he recognized whoever it was, he leaned forward to murmur in my ear. "Your friend is coming."

I looked toward where he gestured, expecting to see one of Eliza's many high school acquaintances. Instead, I saw… *me.* My inner mind rebelled, unable to comprehend what I was seeing. I recognized that jean-jacket, those leggings, those sneakers. I remembered wearing that exact outfit, this exchange we had outside her locker. I instinctively shrunk back in Eliza's mind. This was too weird, I couldn't process it fast enough.

"Hey, Vanessa!" Eliza called to me, waving. *Wait a minute,* I realized. *I hadn't made Eliza say that.* I was sitting at the back of her mind, frozen by the inability to understand what I was witnessing. But if I wasn't controlling Eliza, then who was?

"Hey, Eliza!" other-me called, stepping toward us. "Ready for that bio quiz?"

I—the real me—remembered this conversation. I had walked up to Eliza, asking about the bio quiz, and she had changed the topic to—

"No, but I am ready for lunch today! It's Friday, and you know what that means."

"Mac and cheese!" Other-me smiled. "Best day of the week."

Eliza laughed with me, shifting the backpack on her shoulders. "Of course. I'll see you later, then?"

"Of course!" The other-me waved, moving to walk back down the hallway. "I'll leave you two alone for now. Talk to you later."

I watched myself turn and walk away down the hall. This all felt so wrong. Still too freaked out to take over again, I allowed Eliza to finish the conversation with Trevor without me.

"I should probably get to class," Eliza said. "See you block four?"

"Of course." Trevor brushed a piece of Eliza's hair away from her face and tucked it behind her ear. "I hope you come to the party tomorrow. I think it'll be fun."

Eliza nodded, biting her lip. After one last long kiss that made me shrivel up with embarrassment, Trevor also moved away and disappeared into the crowd.

The warning bell sounded, and just like that, I was back in control. My stomach churned as I watched Trevor's retreating figure. Well, now I knew that I didn't need to be in control all the time. Eliza had the ability to take the wheel whenever I stepped back. It seemed there were rules to—whatever this was I was living.

I forced myself to focus back on Eliza's locker. Here was an opportunity to try it out. Placing my right hand on the lock, I mentally stepped back again and pictured Eliza's hand turning the dial. Without hesitation, Eliza put in her combination. A few seconds later, the lock released and the door swung open.

Huh. Not bad. I hung Eliza's backpack on the hook, and after confirming her first class was English, I started to pull out her books. But I paused. Something colorful caught my eye, behind a binder on the top shelf. I lifted it and froze as the object came into focus.

There was a teething ring in Eliza's locker, a ring made of tiny jelled circles. It looked like it was already used, with subtle teeth marks pressed into the gummy material. *What the hell? What was that doing in there?* I reached out to touch it and as soon as I did, I felt something shift. Before I could process what was happening, the world around me faded to black, and I was somewhere else.

ൾ

"Here ya go!" My voice was high, squeaky. Although I was standing up, I was too close to the floor. It wasn't the school floor though. It was wooden, scratched and worn. There was a child crawling toward me, a girl. The first strands of dark hair were beginning to appear, and someone had tied them up so it splayed out like a little fountain at the top of her head. I reached out, handing the soft ring to her. She grabbed it, chomping down with as much strength as she could muster.

Sitting down beside the child, I explained, "You need to get your teeth so you can eat big-girl food. Like me!" The baby stared at me, drool dripping from the side of her mouth. She giggled, seemingly at nothing. Reaching out, I patted the top of her head. "You're a good baby sister."

ൾ

I blinked, gasping as the familiar sights and sounds of high school bombarded my senses once more. A few passersby threw me strange looks, but no one questioned my exclamation. I glanced down at the toy, turning it over in my hand.

"What the *hell* is going on?"

III

THE REST OF the school day passed in a blur. Now that I realized Eliza could take over, I allowed her to do so whenever possible. I was still pretty spooked from whatever I had seen when I touched the teething ring, but I didn't have the mental capacity to contemplate what that could mean at the moment. Besides, it was a lot easier to let Eliza come up with her own interesting catchphrases than for me to come up with my own. I was still clinging to the belief that maybe this was something that would just wear off after a while, that I would wake up and be Vanessa again. But if I was really honest with myself, the more time I spent in Eliza's mind, the less sure I became that this was actually a dream. Does a dream within a dream happen? Then what was that thing when I saw when I touched the teething ring? And if it wasn't a dream, though, then what was it?

As I watched Eliza move through her day, I tried to mentally work out what happened with the vision. The most straightforward answer seemed to be that it was simply one of Eliza's memories. But from what I could tell, Eliza didn't know anything about the child. I guess it can be hard to tell babies apart, though, so maybe she just didn't recognize her. Even so, Eliza came from a blond-haired, blue-eyed family. None of the cousins or extended relatives of hers I had met had anything close to dark hair. And the girl in the vision specifically said "sister." So I'm thinking it probably wasn't one of Eliza's relatives, meaning it probably wasn't one of her memories. While I did have black hair, no one in my family had had a baby in the last few years. So I didn't think it was one of my memories. The teething ring didn't help clear anything up either. There was no name on it or other identifying features, at least from what I could see. I would've thought it was weird being in Eliza's locker by itself, even without the strange vision that accompanied it. I slipped it into Eliza's backpack and decided to keep it there until I figured out what to do with it. Who knew? Maybe it would come in handy later.

In the end, I decided to continue with the rest of the school day. Hopefully, if I ignored all the weird stuff that was happening, everything would just go back to the way it was. Not that the life I was used to was all that great, but it was better than relieving someone else's. At the moment, there was nothing I could do except continue living as Eliza until this wore off (or I woke up) and I was Vanessa again. So I gritted my teeth, steeled my shoulders, and prepared myself for a day as Eliza.

I watched as my friend discussed the French Revolution in history, took notes during calc, and ate her lunch with other-me. Although this was my first day living (quite literally) in her shoes, I imagined most of her days were like this: just going through the motions, chatting with friends, sharing sweet moments with Trevor. I hoped she'd appreciated everything she'd had before it was all taken away.

The day passed quickly, and soon enough, Eliza was back home, drudging through homework. After two hours of watching Eliza study for a history test she would never take, I finally stepped forward and mentally told her it was time for sleep. I didn't feel tired physically, but I was emotionally drained. As I moved to slip under the sheets and close my eyes, I realized for the first time how truly crazy this all was. I was living in my friend's mind, experiencing her life, her thoughts. It all seemed wrong. I snuggled closer to the blankets, praying that sleep would take me under its wing. I didn't want to do this anymore. It broke me to hear Eliza's voice, to see her interacting with people, knowing that it was all so fragile. When I woke up again, all this would be gone. Eliza would still be missing, and none of this reenactment would matter. At this point, I was just drawing out the inevitable. I needed to wake up and get back to reality. Reliving the past wouldn't save Eliza.

When I resurfaced again, my eyes remained shut, but I knew that I had slept for some time. I breathed a sigh of relief into the darkness. It was over. I was Vanessa again. The nightmare was behind me. Now that I was back to reality, I could continue working on bringing Eliza home. I opened my eyes, sparked with a new determination. But what I saw sent my heart tumbling down, pulse spiraling out of control.

"No." I breathed, peeling off the covers and rubbing my eyes. When I opened them again, to my horror, the sight remained the same. "No no no no no…"

I was still in Eliza's bedroom. I stood up and rushed to the bathroom, desperately flicking on the lights and staring at the mirror. I was *still* Eliza. I pressed both hands to the counter and leaned over the sink. My breaths came quick and raspy as sharp, jagged panic set in.

This wasn't a dream. You don't fall asleep in a dream and then wake up again. Wasn't that, like, a *rule* in dreams? So what was going on? And why was it happening to me? My mind was spinning, thoughts traveling faster than I could keep up with. With much difficulty, I forced myself to slow it down and think things through rationally—or at least with as much rationality as I could muster.

If this wasn't a dream, then… did that mean this was real? No, that couldn't be true. Maybe I was reliving a memory, one of Eliza's. If this was a memory, then that meant this was all taking place in my head (or Eliza's, I guess). So nothing I was doing was actually happening—I was just watching the memory like a movie.

There was another option, though, one that scared me more than I cared to admit. What if I was reliving the *past*? Like not a memory but the *actual* past? How was that even possible? I'd seen movies about time travel, and they rarely ended well for the traveler. The characters usually ended up trying to change the past, which affected all sorts of stuff in the future.

Change the past.

The thought straightened my spine, and my eyes shot open. If I was right in believing that this *was* the past, then *maybe* I had some say in how all this turned out. I could *control* Eliza. *That meant*—I nearly gasped aloud as I realized—*I could stop her from going missing.*

In one last desperate attempt, I reached my right hand over to my left and pinched the back of my hand. Nope.

Definitely awake. And if by stroke of crazy, insane luck my hypothesis about this whole thing was true, that meant I had been given a second chance—a chance to save my friend from whatever fate befell her that night at the party. I swallowed past the lump in my throat, pushed back the tears. This wasn't a time for weakness. I needed to be strong—for Eliza.

I had work to do.

If I was going to pull this off, the first thing I needed was time—time to lay out everything I knew, time to figure out my next step. Flicking my gaze toward a clock hanging on the far wall, I realized it was nearly 6:00 a.m. Mrs. Barrows would come in any minute to wake Eliza up for school.

But I wasn't going to school today. Now, I had a plan.

I grabbed a washcloth from the cabinet and soaked it in hot water. After wringing it out until it stopped dripping, I went back to bed and draped it over my face. The hot cloth laid heavily over my eyes as the blood rushed to my face. Once everything was in place, I waited.

A few minutes later, Mrs. Barrows knocked on the bedroom door. Just as the door began to creak open, I scrunched up the cloth and shoved it under the covers. It left my face burning and my cheeks red, cloaked in a damp sheen of what appeared to be sweat. Not my best fake-out work, but it would have to do on short notice.

"Good morning, sweetheart," Mrs. Barrows whispered. I watched her out of the corner of my eye as she walked up to the side of my bed and stood over my still figure."

I slowly opened my eyes halfway, careful not to focus on anything in particular. "Morning, Mom."

Mrs. Barrows' voice went from warm greeting to concerned adult in an instant. "You don't look so good." Operating on maternal instinct, she gently touched the back of her hand to my forehead. She drew it away, clicking her tongue. "Uh oh, you feel warm. Do you think you have a fever?"

"Maybe," I croaked, letting out a dry cough. All the times I had watched *Ferris Bueller's Day Off* were about to pay off.

Mrs. Barrows pressed her lips into a thin line of concern. "Maybe you should take the day off. Do you have any big tests or anything in school?"

I shook my head, ignoring the major history test that Eliza and I had both been studying the night before. With a jolt, I realized that Eliza hadn't been in class for that test. She had stayed home from school sick, just like I was doing. I was still following the path Eliza had taken before she went missing. I cursed myself for not realizing it sooner. How could I have forgotten? But it was too late to turn back now. It wasn't like I could magically get rid of a fever. Besides, with the full day ahead of me, I had plenty of time to figure out how to get her to miss the party. There was a still a chance I could cheat destiny.

"Well, that's a relief. I'll call you out today." Mrs. Barrows tucked the sheets closer to my face, worry etching her features. "You deserve a day off. You've been working so hard this year." She started to move away but groaned and turned back to look at me. "I almost forgot, I have the double shift today. I'm not going to be home until late. Will you be okay by yourself all day?"

"Mm hm," I murmured, allowing my eyes to flutter shut. *Wow, that was easier than I thought.*

Mrs. Barrows stood there for a moment, and I was afraid she had seen through my hoax. But then I heard her walk to the doorway. "Okay, sweetie. I'll let you rest," she whispered.

"Don't you worry 'bout a thing. Just focus on getting better. And don't hesitate to text me if you need something. Okay?"

"Mm hm."

A few seconds later, the door closed behind her. I wiped the condensation from my face with my sleeve and tossed the damp rag into the laundry bin across the room. I waited for several minutes, but I could still hear Mrs. Barrows putzing around the kitchen. Finally, desperate from something to distract my mind, I pulled out Eliza's phone and logged on to my own social media. I didn't feel comfortable looking through Eliza's. After scrolling on Instagram for an hour or so, I heard the garage door open and close. I waited another ten minutes, just to be sure. Then, satisfied I was alone, I got to work.

The first thing I did was grab a pencil and paper. I needed to write down everything I remembered about the night Eliza went missing. I wanted to be as prepared as possible for the coming day. Luckily, Eliza's disappearance was all I had been thinking about for the last several months, going over every detail, day after day. It didn't take me long to come up with the general outline as to how it all went down.

1. Eliza had stayed home from school that day. She told everyone she was sick, but now I'm pretty certain she stayed home for other reasons (mainly me). Or maybe she saw the weird dream/vision thing too when she opened her locker. At this point, it was hard to tell, her memories getting jumbled with my own. It was getting hard to tell which was which.

2. Eliza was asked to a party that night. She said yes. This was the party Trevor had been talking about. I wasn't invited to the party, but Eliza was. I couldn't remember anyone mentioning Eliza didn't want to go, but I just saw firsthand that Trevor could be pretty insistent.

3. Eliza made it to the party, left alone around midnight, and disappeared. Witnesses claimed that she decided to drive herself home after Trevor wanted to stay longer, but she never made it back to her house. Something happened to her between the party and her house.

Once I had finished writing, I looked everything over again. The answer seemed simple enough. To make sure Eliza didn't go missing, she couldn't go to that party. And since I had already committed myself to the "sick day," the excuse was already in place. Nobody wanted a sick girl crashing their party. My plan was solid. Eliza would miss the party, and no one would be the wiser to the real reason why. Even if everything didn't end up going exactly as I hoped, it felt good to have at least the outline of plan.

With my decision made, even if it was based on conjecture, I realized I had nothing else to do for the rest of the day. As long as I kept up the facade of being sick, I was all set. Heading downstairs, I ate a small breakfast and made myself a cup of coffee. Having the day to myself was nice, but seeing as I was in the wrong house, there wasn't much for me to do. I eventually settled on watching a movie to pass the time. I scrolled through hundreds of films on Netflix before settling on the original *Iron Man*. It wasn't my favorite, but it provided enough mindless entertainment and tongue-in-cheek jokes to fill the tense silence.

As I sat there, half-watching the television, I started thinking. What would happen after this? Would everything go back to normal once I saved Eliza? What if it didn't? Would I be Eliza *forever*? I rubbed my head, attempting to massage away the beginning of a headache. I couldn't perseverate on that. This existential stuff was giving me a migraine. I steered my thoughts back to the movie, trying not to think too far into the future.

By lunchtime, I had made it through the first two *Iron Man* movies and started the third. Beginning to get antsy, I suddenly remembered Eliza's phone. I needed to check and make sure she didn't miss any messages. It was unlike Eliza to leave any text unread for more than five minutes.

I found it where I left it earlier that morning, charging next to her bed. As soon as I pressed the power button, I saw a slew of new messages, mostly from Mrs. Barrows, asking how Eliza was doing. I answered those first, making sure to add the cheesy sick emojis that parents just eat up. I got a reply less than a minute later, reminding me to drink lots of water and take Advil.

There were a few Instagram notifications from Eliza's account, a bunch of generic college e-mails—and a text from Trevor.

Trevor: babe where u at?

Looking at the time stamp, I realized he had sent it earlier this morning, probably when he didn't see Eliza at her locker. I texted him back.

Eliza: at home sick :p

It took a few minutes for him to respond. I figured he was

trying to find a time to text when he wasn't at risk of being seen by a teacher.

Trevor: r u really sick tho lol

I started to text back a confirmation, *Yes, I really am*, but suddenly, my fingers froze. I couldn't text anything.

"What the…" I breathed, staring at my hands. I tried to type a "Y," but nothing happened. I couldn't move. I felt myself being pushed, pulled, *dragged* to the back of her mind. This wasn't part of the plan. Why I wasn't in control anymore?

And then much to my horror, Eliza began to type a response.

"No," I said, louder now. I fought with every fiber of my being against my friend. "No, you're sick." As soon as she hit send, I suddenly gained control again. I gasped, holding the phone to my face.

Eliza: nah, just faking. had to study for history :/

I strained with all my might, trying to force Eliza to type back something, *anything* to reverse what had been said. *No, I'm actually sick. I'm not faking it.* But as soon as I tried to, I was forced out of the spotlight again. Trevor texted back quickly.

Trevor: haha i thought so. you still on for that party tonight?

Eliza: of course. pick me up at 7?

"No—Eliza, you can't go!" Hot tears filled my eyes, blurred my vision, and spilled down my cheeks. Why couldn't I help her? Why couldn't I *save* her? *"You can't go!"*

Trevor: yep. see you tonight :)

I watched helplessly as Eliza sealed her fate.

Eliza: see you <3

I threw the phone onto my bed as sobs wracked my body.

"What's the point?" I cried into to the silence. "Why am I here if I can't even save her? *Why am I here?*" The still air that met my desperate words infuriated me. Seconds ticked on, and my tears continued to fall. Eventually, though, my ragged breathing stilled as my mind slowly cleared.

One last time, I raised my eyes and placed all my pain and sorrow into four whispered words: "Why am I here?"

Again, I was met with silence, but this time the silence held my answer. The response wasn't given in a booming, celestial voice as I had half-expected but rather in a thought that slipped into the back of my mind.

If I was here, reliving all this, then maybe when I did make it back home (*if* I made it back home, said another voice, but I ignored that one) I could *find* her. Even if I couldn't change what had already been done, by witnessing it all through her eyes, maybe I could see something that would help me find her.

I was beginning to understand things. This alternate reality, it seemed to have rules. There were some things that couldn't be changed, I realized that now. I was reliving the past. But I couldn't disrupt an event which consequences influenced the future. It seemed like I had some control over what happened as long as it didn't affect the ultimate outcome. As much as I tried to save Eliza from that fate, I couldn't stop her from going to that party, from going missing. I breathed deeply, lungs expanding and contracting against my tight chest. In that moment, I forced myself to accept the very real possibility that I would have to relive my best friend's disappearance, whether that was by abduction, getting lost, or...

My mind rebelled against finishing that last thought. Eliza was alive. I wouldn't allow myself to think otherwise.

IV

NOW THAT I had a plan, a purpose, I threw away all reservations about privacy. I needed to prepare myself, to keep an eye out for any clue or small detail that might foreshadow the coming events. I searched through her text messages, her DMs, Instagram comments: anything that could contain suspicious activity. If there was foul play involved, I needed to know. Maybe there was something crucial Eliza had missed that I could find.

But as the hours ticked on, it seemed less and less likely that what I was looking for actually existed. There were hundreds of messages to sift through. Most were just mundane communications, nothing suspicious that would lend itself to my makeshift investigation. I slowly became aware of a growing discomfort, and it wasn't until I shut off the phone to rub my eyes that I realized I was hungry—really hungry. I squinted at the pink-trimmed clock hanging above Eliza's door—6:40. Nearly four hours had passed since I started looking through her phone. Where had the time gone?

I turned back to Eliza's cell phone, stopped, then looked at the clock again.

"Six forty?" I exclaimed, leaping to my feet. Trevor was picking me up in twenty minutes. I made a feeble attempt to stop Eliza from getting ready, but it was no use. My friend was in full panic mode. I tried to bring up the fact that her mom could come home any minute and would notice she wasn't home, but Eliza's subconscious reminded me that she worked the late shift tonight and wouldn't return until at least 1:00 a.m. As long as Eliza returned home from the party before then, it would be fine.

I mentally stepped back while Eliza began sifting through her closet. In real life, I didn't understand makeup or fashion or anything considered "feminine." My parents were lucky when they got me to wear the one formal dress I owned for Easter. Even on Christmas, I only ever wore an ugly holiday sweater and jeans. She eventually chose a tightly fit, royal purple dress. It had two strings crossing over her chest in an "X" and barely enough material to make it to her thighs. As she admired herself in the mirror, I sighed. If only I had those curves in real life. I then realized how awkward it was to envy my missing friend and pulled my focus back to Eliza's current task: makeup.

After what seemed like an eternity, Eliza eventually stepped back from the mirror, satisfied. She had applied an expert smoky eye and a deep burgundy lipstick. Her blond hair was tucked into a messy bun that looked both casual and delicate at the same time, a few strands hanging loose around her face.

She looked beautiful.

Her transformation was timed perfectly, for just as she stepped away, her phone buzzed. It was Trevor, parked in front of the house. I decided to take back control and witness as much as I could from the front seat. That way, when the reins were pulled away from me again, I would know something future-changing was happening. I wasn't sure how well that plan would work, but it was worth a try.

Trevor's car was a silver Toyota Corolla. It was small, compact, but seemed to be in pretty good condition. He stepped out, wearing a plain T-shirt and a smile that would easily make any girl go weak in the knees—but not Eliza. She strode right up to him, watching his eyes run up and down her body.

"Wow, babe," he commented softly. "You clean up nice." Trevor kissed Eliza on the lips, hard, and I internally cringed.

I stepped back a little too quickly, saying, "You ready to go?" Luckily, he didn't seem to notice. Or if he did, he didn't comment on it. As I stepped into the car and settled into the passenger seat, the first thing I noticed was the music. "Good song," I said, smiling toward Trevor. "I love the Beatles."

He put the car into reverse, throwing me a strange look. "I think that's the first time you've actually complimented my music."

Oops. I forgot Eliza didn't like classic rock. It must not have been too big a blunder, though, for I was still in control when I responded, "I don't know, the Beatles are beginning to grow on me. I like 'Come Together.'"

"Huh." Satisfied with my response, Trevor turned up the volume. I bobbed my head to the rhythm and looked out the window, watching the houses race by. I spotted three children playing on one of the driveways before the image was whisked away.

The next song was another one of my favorites, Aerosmith's "Love in an Elevator." I had to refrain from singing along, knowing full well Eliza wouldn't know the words. I could've spent the whole night listening to that station. I was impressed by Trevor's choice, it had a good mix of songs. But a few minutes later, we arrived at a large brick house with white-trimmed windows.

The party already seemed to be in full swing. Muted flashes of light could just be seen through the drawn blinds on the second floor, but the pulsating music was far less subtle. The stuff they had playing wasn't nearly as good as what Trevor and I were listening to. From what I could make out, it seemed to be a remix of a pop song that wasn't good to begin with. There seemed to be a steady stream of people entering and exiting through the open front door, the ones going in walking steadily, the ones walking out stumbling.

"Whose house is this again?" I asked, genuinely curious. From what it sounded like from outside, their house was getting trashed. It was pretty large, making me suspect they had a pretty decent income to support it.

"Emma Myers'. Her parents are celebrating their anniversary in Hawaii or something." Trevor turned off the car, staring at the chaos that awaited us inside. "They won't be back for at least a week, so don't stress." He leaned over to grip my hand. "Let's go."

As soon as we walked inside, I knew it was a mistake. Not that it was my decision, but I wondered if Eliza felt the same when she first walked inside. There were people everywhere, leaning against walls, sitting on tables, cross-legged on the floor. The music was so loud I could feel my eardrums vibrating, and I fought the urge to cover them. I spotted at least one beer keg in a corner and a few wine coolers in another. Those seemed to be mostly untouched in comparison to the hard liquor that looked to be almost completely cleared out. A sickly combination of sweet-scented vapor and marijuana smoke filled the air, creating a thick haze over the entire scene.

I swallowed, breathing in the contaminated air. This was going to be a long night. From what I had been told from people who had been here that night, Eliza had stayed until a little after midnight, and then left in Trevor's car. I needed to keep my eyes peeled, ears open, for anything unusual. Binge-watching all twenty seasons of *Law & Order* was about to come in handy.

"Let me get you something to drink!" Trevor shouted, and before I could respond, he disappeared into the mob of people. I stood off to the side, unsure of where to go. Attempting to distract my throbbing head and pounding heart, I busied myself with finding where the music was coming from. At first, it seemed like it was coming from everywhere at once, but I was able to spot at least four speakers in various places around the room, blasting Post Malone. I glanced around at the surround-sound system, gaping windows and ceramic-tiled floors. Wow, these people were rich. Good thing too. Otherwise, there was no way they'd be able to pay for the damage that would undoubtedly be done by the end of tonight.

I was pulled from my thoughts when I felt a tap on my shoulder. I spun around, expecting to see Trevor, but instead, I found myself face-to-face with—

"Dwight?" I shouted over the music. "What do you want?"

"Hey, Elizabeth!" His words were slurred, and I noticed the punch cup in his hand. "Howya doin'?"

I froze for a moment, utterly confused. But when I remembered who I was, I corrected him. "It's Eliza!" Straining my head to look around him, I searched for Trevor. Where was he?

"Ya know…" Dwight took a step forward, the space between us going from slightly uncomfortable to way too close. "You're really pretty."

"Thanks," I muttered, trying to walk backward, but the wall of people behind me prevented me from moving more than a few inches. Hoping he'd get the hint, I asked pointedly, "Hey, have you seen *Trevor*?"

Either not hearing or not caring about my question, he reached out a hand to grip my arm. "Maybe we should hang out sometime."

"Ew!" I couldn't control the exclamation as I pried his fingers off me. He seemed more confused than angry as I prepared my response, but luckily, I was cut off when a familiar voice called to me.

"Eliza!" I glanced to the right, relief washing over me when I spotted Eliza's boyfriend pushing toward me through the crowd. Completely ignoring Dwight, I shoved myself between people until I was by his side. Eliza probably would've handled the situation much more gracefully, but I just had to get out of there.

Trevor laughed as he handed me a Solo cup, looking back at Dwight's despondent expression. "You need me to beat him up for you? 'Cause I'll do it."

"Nah," I replied, rolling my eyes. "He's so drunk, he doesn't even realize what he's doing." I glanced down at the orange liquid Trevor had passed me. "What is this?"

"A screwdriver," he responded. "Orange juice and vodka. It's the only drink I know how to make."

I nodded, not wanting to wear out my voice from all the

yelling. I decided to just hold it in my hand and not drink any. It was better to stay sober so I could keep my mind clear. After a few minutes, though, I felt Eliza taking over. Much as I fought against it, she brought the cup to her lips. I shivered as the tangy sweet drink flooded my taste buds. This was Eliza's first mistake. I never thought of her as someone who would get wasted at some party, but I could feel the smoke and music dulling her senses. With every sip she took, the night slipped further and further away from her.

As the night wore on, I felt myself getting pushed further and further back into Eliza's conscious. Every time she put the Solo cup back to her mouth again, I tried to force her hands to stop but to no avail. What was she thinking? Maybe that was the problem: She wasn't thinking. It broke me to see her like this, getting wasted, drinking away the night. I could barely see through her eyes, the alcohol fogging her gaze and clogging her senses while she played beer pong and danced with various friends.

If only she knew what was coming. If only she knew the pain she would cause others. If only she knew what this night would cost her.

If she knew, she never would have come.

Eventually, I gained back control just long enough to remind her to check the time. Her clumsy fingers reached into her back pocket, withdrawing the cellphone. She blinked hard, the numbers swimming in front of her eyes before finally coming into focus.

"Oh shit," Eliza muttered, turning to Trevor. She tapped him on the shoulder, but he didn't respond. He had his back turned to her, facing the DJ and dancing along to the

EDM. “Trevor!” It took several repetitions of this before he turned around.

Even through the smog and her inebriated gaze, I could tell he was just as drunk as Eliza was. He blinked slowly as his head nodded forward and jolted back up. “What?” he slurred, voice mellow and blurred with alcohol.

Eliza reached out to grip his shoulder, not as a form of affection, but to steady herself as the room shifted around her. “It’s after midnight.”

“No, it’s not!” Trevor shouted, pulling out his phone only slightly more gracefully than Eliza did. He squinted at it. “Yes, it is.”

“I have to—” Eliza paused when a couple shoved past her, arms wrapped around each other. She pushed them away, yelling at them to get a room before repeating, “I have to get home. My mom… she’ll be back soon.”

“Whatever.” Trevor turned around to continue talking to his jock friends, breaking her hold on him, but she tugged him back to face her.

“I need a car to get home.”

He pulled out his keys and shoved them into her open hand. “There. You happy now?”

“But…” Eliza squinted him. “How will you get home?”

“I dunno, you ask too many questions.” Trevor turned around again and screamed, “This song freaking sucks! Change it!”

His cry aroused a chorus of shouts. Soon the room was filled with shouts of “Change it! Change it! Change it!”

With great effort on my part, I forced Eliza to step away. I was still in control, but I could tell my grip was fragile. It wouldn’t be long before I was pushed back again. Things were moving quickly now, and I knew what was coming. How everything gotten out of my control so fast? Stumbling toward the door, I was just able to pull it open and close it behind me. My head pounded, the loud music and alcohol taking its toll.

In the house, it had been easy to lean on people and walls to get around. Now that I was outside, in the open air, I realized how drunk Eliza actually was. Barely able to walk straight, she tripped over a seam in the concrete and almost fell. I allowed her to take a moment to compose herself before forcing her to keep walking. Trevor's car was right in front of us, only a few feet away. All we had to do was get there then drive the fifteen minutes home, and we would be safe. The beginnings of hope fluttered in the back of my mind. Maybe I was wrong. Maybe there was still time to change this.

C'mon, Eliza, I willed her mentally. *Just make it to the car.*

When I reached the driver's side door, I couldn't help but breathe a sigh of relief. I had made it. Now all I had to do was open it, get inside, and close the door behind me. I lifted the keyring to my face and stared hard at it, trying to decipher the buttons. Finally, my thumb found the unlock symbol. The car's lights flashed in confirmation, the doors clicking softly. My hand was on the handle when I heard a voice.

"Honey, are you all right?" The woman sounded concerned, quiet, controlled. If I hadn't known better, I would've thought she was just a worried adult. But knowing what I did, her words set off every alarm bell in my head.

Don't turn around, I ordered Eliza. *Open the car door and get inside.* She ignored me and faced the figure standing behind her. Although the voice was distinctly feminine, she had the hood of her coat up, and I couldn't make out any defining features through the shadows cast over her face. Eliza's current state of mind didn't help, the world tilting and shifting around us.

"Yeah," I managed, attempting to sound as forceful as possible. "I'm fine."

I started to turn back around, but there was a hand on my shoulder. "No, you're not." I looked back, and the woman was right there. I tried to make out her face, but everything was so blurry. And I was so tired…

"You're drunk," the woman insisted. "Here, let me drive you home. That way, you won't get into any more trouble."

No! I screamed at Eliza. *Don't go!*

Eliza paused, and for a moment, I thought she heard me. But then she drooped her head down in what could be taken as a nod.

No, no, no —

"Okay. Come here, honey." There were two hands on my shoulders now, steering me away from Trevor's car. Before I realized it, the woman's hand slipped into mine and the car key was gone. "Everything's gonna be all right, I'm here."

Go back! Turn around! Eliza, please!

My screams never reached her consciousness. I wasn't in control anymore. I had no choice but to watch Eliza be led away. The concrete turned to grass and then to gravel. I turned over my shoulder to see the house disappearing in the distance.

"Where're we go'n?" Eliza mumbled, tripping again.

The woman's grip tightened. "We're just walking to my car. Then I'll drive you home."

Eventually, the van came into sight. I stared at it, trying to make out any defining features, but it was dark and hard to make out in the light. From what I could see, it was boxy and large, with wide curves and dark windows. Its lights flashed yellow against the red paint when the woman unlocked it.

"Here you go," she cajoled, opening the rear door of the car. "Hop in. You'll be home soon."

"Eliza!" I begged one last time. But she wasn't listening.

Eliza staggered into the car, collapsing like a ragdoll across the back row of seats. Her eyelids fluttered. She was so tired. She laid her head down on the soft leather. I tried to force her eyes open, but I was far away.

This was it, I realized. Eliza was getting kidnapped, and I hadn't learned anything about what happened. I don't think she even knew where she was. How could I?

No, she couldn't fall asleep. It couldn't end like this. I needed to see who took her, who abducted my friend. I pounded against the back of her mind, screaming, begging, *pleading* for Eliza to stay awake. It was all pointless. Ignoring my cries, Eliza's eyes closed.

And then there was darkness.

V

AS I RESURFACED back to consciousness, I became aware of several things. First, I could tell that time had passed, more than a few minutes, at least a couple of hours. Second, I was not in the car anymore. I was warm, a little too warm, a thin layer of sweat coating my face. There was a blanket on me. It was heavy and constricting, so I pushed it to the floor. A billow of fresh air brushed my skin, and I opened my eyes.

An impenetrable darkness surrounded me. I squinted around the room while I waited for my eyes to adjust. This was not what I expected being kidnapped would be like. In the movies, the actors had always been bound by rope or zip ties or had their mouths covered in duct tape. And they were usually in some sort of basement or empty room. But I could make out a doorway in front of me with a bookcase on either side, indistinguishable objects filling their shelves. It looked like I was in a bedroom.

Weird.

"Hello?" I whispered, then paused. Wow, my voice was really horse. I must've screwed it up worse than I thought last night. It was all deep and raspy. I cleared it, then spoke again. "Where am I?" That *really* wasn't Eliza's voice. It sounded different, almost as if…

I reached off to my right searching for a cell phone. I grasped it in my hand and struggled to find the power button. The screen flashed to life, blinding me. I groaned (*What the hell did I do to her voice?*) and waited for my eyes to adjust.

8:26 a.m. February 12.

I stopped, read it again.

February 12. I had been asleep for *three months*? That didn't make any sense. When my eyes traveled to the home screen, I saw a picture of a stranger, a twenty-something-year-old guy. He was standing in front of a red pickup truck, and the smirk on his face told the camera he thought he owned the world. It definitely wasn't Trevor or anyone else that I recognized.

This wasn't Eliza's phone. I turned on the device's flashlight, shining it around the room. None of it looked familiar, not the death metal posters on the wall or the stack of *Cloak and Dagger* comics on the shelf.

This wasn't Eliza's room. Where was I?

The beam of light caught a mirror on the wall to the left, directing it back into my eyes. I redirected the glare before standing and walking toward it. I stifled a curse when I stubbed my toe on something hard and pointed. I stopped just long enough to read the cover of a liberal arts textbook before I took the final steps to stand in front of the reflective surface.

I saw messy black hair and dark brown eyes. I saw sharp cheekbones and hunched shoulders. I saw scruff and a protruding Adam's apple.

I saw… *a man*.

PART TWO

Tony

I

I TILTED MY head to the side, blinking hard. The disheveled twenty-something-year-old guy in the mirror did the same.

"Oh, *hell* no," I hissed, cringing when his voice cracked. Nope. I was *not* doing this. I tossed my head back, glaring at the ceiling. "You think this is funny? The Eliza thing was weird enough, but who the *hell am I now*?" Looking back toward the mirror, I took in the wrinkled shirt, droopy eyes, greasy hair. "Am I supposed to know this pothead? 'Cause I don't! How is this a part of Your plan?" I half-expected lightning to come down to strike me for my insolence, but I couldn't care less. This was absolutely ridiculous.

Once my freak-out had run its course, I slowly backed away from the mirror and sat down on Eliza's, I mean, *his* bed. My palms were sweating, and I could feel the air pressing down on my chest. I rested my elbows on my knees, cupped my face in both hands, and focused on breathing. *This was too much to process,* way *too much to process.* The pounding eventually faded from my ears, and I was able to think straight again.

I had assumed that if I didn't wake up as myself when

I went to sleep as Eliza, then I surely would after she got abducted. There was no reason for me to relive any more of this. Eliza had been taken. I hadn't been able to stop it. And come to think of it, I hadn't been able to learn anything more about her disappearance either.

"So why am I a freaking guy?!"

"Tony!" The shrill cry that came from outside my door resulted in my nearly jumping out of my skin—or I guess *his* skin. This was all so confusing. I was so startled that I actually jumped back mentally, melting into the back of his mind just like I had when I had been Eliza.

"Whaddya want, Ma?" he shouted back. To fully understand the conversation that I heard next, imagine the following interaction as being screamed at the top of your lungs.

"You're gonna be late for school!" Her accent was Italian, thick and drawling.

"I'm not goin' to school today!"

"What? Whatsa matta' with you? You sick?"

"I gotta sleep!"

"Holy Mary, Mother of Gawd, how much sleep does one man need?"

"I'm not goin' to school!"

"Your father only sleeps four hours a night! You sleep ten, and you want more! It's just not right!"

"Shut up!"

"I tell you, it's not right! Get outta bed right now, or I'm callin' your father!"

"I do what I want!"

"Sweet Jesus, why did you give me such a lazy son?"

He didn't seem to have a response to that. As he turned away from the closed door to lie back down in bed, I heard his mother, Mrs.—Giordano, Tony's subconscious provided—grumbling to herself in Italian. I watched through Tony's eyes as he pulled out his phone and started scrolling through iFunny. While he wasted time and chuckled at dead memes, I started thinking. Somehow I started to piece things together. It seemed that I was picking this up a little quicker the second time around.

So all this was happening again, for seemingly no reason. At first, I thought that I was experiencing this weird body-time-travel thing because of Eliza's disappearance. But how did this Tony guy have anything to do with my friend? Was there something that tied them together? I thought about it for a moment, then froze. What if Tony was the one who kidnapped Eliza? I had heard a woman speaking when Eliza was taken, but she might've had a partner. For a few seconds, I watched Tony scroll. Judging from the accounts he was looking at and the jokes he found funny, I figured there was enough proof to dismiss that theory. From what I could see of this kid, I didn't think he had the brainpower to solve a sudoku, let alone pull off something like that. So it had to be something else. But what?

After over an hour of sitting through memes and mindless YouTube videos, I still hadn't come up with an answer, but I had come up with a plan. This Tony kid might have the luxury to burn through hours at a time sitting on his ass, but I most certainly didn't. I had to get moving.

First, I stepped into the front of Tony's mind again and pressed the home button of his cell. I needed to figure out where the hell I was. Looking at the model of his cell phone, I decided to try something.

"Hey, Siri." The phone vibrated and glowed, waiting for a question. "Where am I?"

After a moment's hesitation, it responded, *"You're in Akron, Ohio."*

"Akron?" I read and reread the response. That was hundreds of miles away from my hometown, a few hours by car. Why the hell was I in Akron? That wasn't anywhere near where Eliza was abducted. I didn't care about this kid or freaking Akron. I needed to get *home*.

But even as I thought it, something tickled the back of my mind. Not Tony's mind but my own. This wasn't an accident. I was in Eliza's mind for a reason, to witness her abduction, and I was in Tony's mind for a reason too. The sooner I could figure out why, the sooner I could figure out what I was supposed to do. I opened the camera on the phone and flipped it so it faced Tony. My eyes skimmed the shadow of stubble cloaking his chin, the dark brown eyes and deep bags that hung underneath them. He could possibly be characterized as good looking if he actually put the time in to make himself appear slightly less like a hobo. After a few seconds of struggling to place him, I came to my conclusion that I truly had no connection to him. He was a complete stranger to me. That's not to say he's wasn't connected to Eliza in some way though. In any case, I was apparently doomed to live inside his head for however long this lasted.

I looked down at the grubby clothes he was currently wearing and sighed. An oversized college sweatshirt and stained sweatpants weren't going to work if I planned on leaving the house. Striding to his closet, I threw open the doors. Instantly, the odor of sweat and mud hit me like a wall. "Oh crap," I muttered, stifling a gag as I put a hand up to my mouth. "Tony, you disgusting pig." I took a step back, pulling in a deep lungful of fresh air before leaning back into the pile. Picking out the first unstained shirt and jeans I could find, I flung them on his bed with my breath still held. I didn't allow myself to release it until I slammed the door shut.

Luckily, Tony got the hint and started to change without my help. I did, however, step forward for a moment to avert his eyes while he was changing underwear. This whole living-inside-another-person's-head thing was awkward enough without having to worry about seeing… *that*.

Once Tony had pulled himself together as best as he could—I tried to suggest that he tidy up his hair, but the best I could get him to do was rake a hand through it—I walked to the bedroom door. Pressing my ear against it, I listened to see if his mother was still in the house. The dead silence suggested otherwise. This definitely wasn't the Barrows' household, with its busy scrambled-egg-scented mornings. Satisfied that we were alone, I quietly pushed the door open and stepped out.

There was a girl standing directly in front of the door.

The response was instantaneous. "What the hell, Jackie?" According to Tony's subconscious, this was his sister, more specifically, his twin sister. She was slightly older than him, only by six minutes. But damn it, she made those six minutes count. There was a malevolent glimmer in her chocolate brown eyes. Her style was almost goth in nature, but even with the heavy makeup, she couldn't completely cover her natural beauty.

"I could ask you the same, *An-to-ni-o*," Jackie replied, dragging out each syllable of her brother's name. He narrowed his eyes at her. She smiled, enjoying his discomfort, before raising one dark eyebrow so far up it disappeared under a lock of equally dark hair. "You gave Mom such a hard time this morning, she started screaming at *me* about it. I haven't seen her that mad since you ate the entire antipasto dish before we had the neighbors over."

Tony concealed a smile, choosing instead to say, "Whatever, Jac." He was back in full jerk mode when he added, "I wake up late, I get shit for it. I wake up early, I get shit for it. What do you want me to do?"

"Never wake up," Jackie replied, and Tony cringed. *Oof.* That was rough. If I was in control, I would've laughed, but Tony was too busy trying to formulate a comeback. Not surprisingly, he was unable to think of one in time before Jackie continued, "Well, even though you're running late, you're still up earlier than usual. So you down for helping me cook breakfast?"

Unsure of Tony's cooking skills, I let him respond. "Hell no. I got stuff to do."

Her lips, painted a deep red, curled into a sneer. "Whatever. We all know full well that 'stuff' means *Fortnite* and live chats with—"

"Enough!" Tony growled, pushing past her toward the stairs. "I have to go out, buy some stuff for a science project." Jackie groaned and rolled her eyes. Tony ignored her griping as he descended onto the main floor. As he stepped onto flat ground, he glanced around warily for his mother. Lucky for us, she had already left for her daily rosary at the nearby chapel. I didn't even know they had stuff like that anymore. The entire house smelled like lavender incense, which I guessed was courtesy of Jackie, as it seemed to waft from her room into the rest of the house. Tony ignored Jackie's griping, extracting the car keys out of his jacket pocket and tugging on a pair of tattered Nike sneakers.

"Jerk!" Jackie yelled to my retreating figure. Tony responded by flipping her off.

Ugh, I grumbled mentally. Why was I stuck in the head of such a loser? Why couldn't I be in his sister's mind? She seemed way more interesting.

The homework excuse wasn't completely fabricated. When Tony had brought it up, he immediately remembered the chemistry term paper he had to finish by Friday. Even so, I knew he had no intention of working on it. I just needed an excuse to get out of that house, find some peace and quiet so I could concentrate. Although Tony seemed to have nothing to do with Eliza, I still had a feeling that this whole situation had *everything* to do with her disappearance. I wasn't going to let Tony's lazy nature to get in the way of my solving this thing.

I stepped up to the front door and opened it an inch to savor the last of the house's warmth before I walked out into the crisp February morning. There were two vehicles stationed in the driveway, but it didn't take long to figure out which was Tony's. My two options were a chipped, muddy green car or an obnoxious red truck. Even if I hadn't recognized the latter from his phone's wallpaper, I would have guessed that the truck belonged to my current host. It seemed to fit his personality perfectly: big, loud, and obnoxious.

As I walked toward the icon of masculinity, I noticed something sticking out of the door handle. At first, I thought it was a reflection on the spotless exterior, but as I stepped closer, I realized it was something else, something small. A toy. The red paint blended with the color of the truck, and

I didn't realize it was a little car until I was standing a few steps away.

The toy was obviously used, paint chipped in some areas, and the fender bent above the wheels. I tried to pull it out of the handle, but when I touched it, I felt a falling sensation, and the world faded around me.

It was happening again, I realized. I was about to relive another memory. And just as that fact set in, it began.

⁂

The light shone through the windows, bright and clear, reflecting off the blue linoleum of the kitchen floor. I lay on my stomach, legs splayed out behind me, one hand propping up my chin. My right hand clutched the red car as I moved it along the edges of the tile.

"Vroom, vroom," I garbled, the new word fun to shape in my mouth.

"That's right," a rumbling, masculine voice replied. I looked up to see a tall man sitting across from me. His dark hair was short and spiky, and a smile stretched up to his eyes. "A car says, 'Vroom, vroom.'"

⁂

I blinked and everything vanished as the world faded back into view. My legs felt wobbly beneath me, and I pressed a palm against the window of the truck for support. It had happened again—another vision or memory or whatever the hell it was. I searched for some connection in Tony's mind, an explanation as to where this came from. But just like Eliza, he had no idea about the origins of the toy or the memory. A strange sense of deja vu fell over me, like I should know where the car was from. But I didn't. I had absolutely no idea about any of it. It was almost as if the vision was someone else's memories, not Eliza's or Tony's.

As I stood there, eyes squeezed shut against the pounding in my ears, a wave of helplessness swept over me. I was going in circles. All of this was happening again. I woke up in someone else's mind, began to relive their day, found a mysterious toy, and experienced a memory that wasn't mine. All of this had already occurred with Eliza, but I still had no explanation for any of it. I wouldn't be surprised if Tony was—

My eyes widened as I clutched the toy. There was the connection I had been looking for. I wouldn't know until it was too late, but if I was right, then that meant that there *was* something tying Eliza and Tony together. Not a family relation or an object but an event. And I was pretty sure I knew what was going to happen next, the understanding of which shook me to my core.

Just like Eliza, Tony was going to get abducted.

II

"WELL," I MUTTERED as the realization washed over me. "I am totally screwed." I had a feeling that someone would try to abduct Tony, but unlike Eliza, I had no idea when or how it was going to happen. It was like knowing the answer to a question on a test without knowing which question the answer was matched to. All the information I had been gathering throughout this whole ordeal had started to seem pointless, like no matter what I did, the result would always be the same. And there was still the chance that I was completely wrong about this whole Tony-abduction thing. Maybe Eliza and Tony were connected in a different way, a way I hadn't thought of yet. Even so, I decided to assume it as a sure thing that Tony would be taken. Best case scenario, I was wrong and Tony wouldn't get abducted. Worst case scenario… I shivered at the thought. Better to plan for the worst, just to be safe. Not that he would appreciate me saving his sorry ass.

I had plans to do some serious research about Eliza and Tony, and that meant there was no way I could go back in that house. Tony's subconscious told me it was very unusual for him to actually be doing homework, which meant if I tried to use it as a cover-up for what I was *really* working on, Jackie and their mom would ask way too many questions. I needed somewhere I could think in private, without the threat of prying eyes. I wasn't familiar with Akron, but Tony was. Maybe he could actually come in handy.

Closing my eyes, I whispered, "Okay. We need to go someplace quiet and alone. Where can we go?" Tony thought about it for a moment, a very long moment, before he came up with a diner. No, a diner has too many people. Option number two was McDonalds. That was even worse. "C'mon," I whispered. "Think." Another few seconds passed before he finally came up with—"Chuck E. Cheese?" I groaned. "What are you, five? Is all you think about *food?* What about a library, you dweeb? Huh? Where's the nearest library?" I wasn't at all shocked when he couldn't tell me how to get to the library, so I resorted to using his phone. Tony's mind inwardly rebelled at my choice of location, longing for the warm, welcoming covers of his bed, but I convinced him that he needed to go to the library to start on the chemistry project. He didn't need to know that I had no intention of even opening a chemistry textbook. Lucky for him.

The library was a small cozy place, much like the rest of the town. When I walked inside, I looked up and down the shelves of books. The whole place smelled of yellowed pages and stale ink, a scent only a room of old books can produce. I breathed it in, the familiar scent a comfort, but inner-Tony recoiled from it. Loser.

A woman sat in a rocking chair off to one side with three children sitting at her feet, enraptured by the story she read. Pausing for a moment, I watched them. There were two girls and a boy, all wide eyes and big ears as they absorbed every word the woman spoke. It was such a pure, authentic moment that I had a hard time looking away. I almost wished I could be a part of it, totally focused on the story, with no understanding of the horrors of reality.

I forced my eyes away and spotted a vacant table housing a collection of dated computers off to the left. Aside from a few other patrons milling about, the rest of the main room was almost completely empty. I was confused until I looked at the clock on the wall above the return desk. It was 9:30 a.m. People weren't exactly rushing to get to the library the minute it opens on a Tuesday morning.

I sat down in front of the nearest computer and flicked on the power switch. While it booted up, I went to a nearby employee and asked for a pencil and some paper. I opened the search drive as soon as the desktop loaded and was about to start typing in Eliza's name when I felt Tony prod me from the back of his mind. I couldn't just start working on my own project without giving him something to do. I still wasn't sure how this whole out-of-body thing worked, but there was no way he was going to let me research for hours without giving him something to occupy his mind. Resigning myself to some lost time, I stepped back and ordered Tony to begin working on his paper.

After putzing around on the computer for a quarter of an hour and it was clear he wouldn't get any further without a little guidance, I took back control and typed his topic—chemical engineering—into Google. He eventually found a site or two that looked like they could be useful. Moving as slow as molasses, he opened up a Word document and copy-pasted the articles inside. He almost forgot citations, but I reminded him just in time. Once he clicked the print button, he stood, stretched, then meandered to the printer to retrieve his paper. When he returned to the table and proceeded to pull out his phone from his sweatshirt pocket, I realized that this was the grand total of work that Tony was going to complete while we were at the library. What transpired took a total of seventeen minutes.

As I prepared to move back to the front of his mind, I swear to God, he yawned. “Oh please,” I whispered, shoving his phone back into his sweatshirt and turning back to the computer. “You are *not* allowed to yawn after that pathetic research attempt.” Now it was time for the real work. Clicking the cursor back into the search bar, I quickly typed, “Eliza Barrows disappearance.”

There was a part of me wondering if, in this past I was reliving, the articles written about Eliza would be different from what I remembered. But no, they were exactly the same. I had hoped that by some stroke of genius, all the facts that seemed irrelevant would click into place after I witnessed her disappearance myself, but nothing did. Even though I could practically quote the articles after all the times I had read them, I looked them over again word by word to see if there was anything I had missed. There was a party, no witnesses, and everyone thought she drove home until her parents couldn’t find her the next morning. Trevor’s car was still there in the morning, but his keys were nowhere to be found.

There was no mention of the minivan, or the woman, in any of the articles.

To be honest, I wasn’t really surprised. Eliza was the only one outside when she had approached her. There was no one else there to see the woman, and an old car would definitely blend into a street filled with the vehicles of partying teenagers.

I closed my eyes, trying to reimagine every detail. It had been so dark and difficult to see through the haze of alcohol, but I distinctly remembered the car being large and red. Much as I tried, I couldn't remember if I saw a brand. It wasn't like I could search "large red minivan" and instantly come up with the exact make and model, but it was a starting point. The woman was trickier. Her face had been almost completely concealed by shadows, so all I had to go on was her voice. There was nothing particularly outstanding about it. I guessed from the deeper, raspy tenor that she was middle-aged, but it was hard to tell by just her whispered words. She could've been way younger and a chain-smoker, which would have resulted in the same effect. I couldn't shake the sense that there was something familiar about her, but just like the toys and the rest of this whole shitty escapade, I couldn't figure out what.

A woman with a run-down, red minivan—that's all I had to go on for Eliza. But I had even less for Tony's predicted abduction. I started typing "Tony Giordano disappearance" into the browser but stopped myself. Tony hadn't even disappeared yet, so there wouldn't be any articles written about him. If it wasn't for me, the unnoticed and unintended extra occupant in Tony's head, there would be no reason to suspect something was wrong.

I felt like I was wasting an opportunity. I had the best seat in the house, witnessing it all from the victim's perspective, but I still couldn't figure out why any of this was happening. I was the only one who could help Tony, and I had absolutely no idea what to do with this guy.

"What am I supposed to do?" I groaned, dropping my head in my hands. My outburst was met with a disapproving look from a librarian filling away books nearby. I gave her an apologetic grimace, then felt a vibration in my pocket. It was a text from Jackie.

Jackie: One of your loser friends just asked me to ask you where you are.

I hesitated before texting back. Should I lie and claim that Tony was at school? After a moment, I decided against it. Maybe honesty was the best policy.

Tony: at the library

Jackie: Haha, very funny. Where are you actually?

I felt Tony get agitated as his mind flooded with thoughts on being "underappreciated" and "undervalued." He was about to write back a snarky response, but I made him pause. On a normal day, it was seriously unlikely that Tony would be at the library doing schoolwork. It wasn't a "normal day" for Tony, but Jackie didn't know that. I had to come up with something realistic that Tony was doing. Even though it was a lie, it was still more believable than the truth of where Tony actually was.

Tony: u caught me. I'm getting the oil changed in my truck

Jackie: I knew it. You never read anymore. I'm not sure you even know how to read.

Tony:... if im texting you back then that means i can read your texts.

Jackie: Okay, you can read texts. But I don't think you have the attention span to read a full book.

Tony: ive read books before

Jackie: Maybe when you were in fourth grade, but not anymore.

Jackie: You know what, prove it. What's the last book you read?

She had Tony backed into a corner, and she knew it. His subconscious told me that she was right, he didn't read anymore. It also told me that the last book he finished was *Fahrenheit 451* in seventh grade. Once he discovered *SparkNotes*, his days of reading cover to cover were over. The only thing he read recently was *Playboy*, and that wasn't exactly A+ reading material.

Tony: the bible?

Jackie: Lol, nice try. Why'd you ditch today, anyway?

Tony: idk i just didn't feel like going to school today

Jackie: Or any day.

Tony: aren't you supposed to be in class

Jackie: I'm in an elective, our teacher doesn't care if we're on our phones.

Tony: whatev. stop bothering me, i got stuff to do.

Jackie: Yeah, like read the Bible.

Tony: maybe i will

Jackie: I'll believe it when I see it.

As Tony rolled his eyes and placed his phone back down, I couldn't help but inwardly chuckle. Jackie had my kind of humor. I was an only child, and I had always wished for a little sister to talk to and joke with. Jackie almost seemed to be the sister I never had. We both had the same twisted sense of humor, the same tongue-in-cheek remarks. Again, I bemoaned the fact that I was stuck in her brother's mind instead of hers. Jackie seemed to be way cooler and more interesting.

After a few more minutes of fruitless searching, I decided to print out all the articles on Eliza that I could find. Chances were they wouldn't reveal anything else to me, but I'd rather have them just in case I was able to piece something together later on. I also looked up some basic self-defense moves with step-by-step diagrams. At this point, I was pretty sure I couldn't change the future. So if Tony was going to get abducted, there was nothing I could do. But if there was even the slightest chance that I could stop it, I wouldn't let the opportunity pass me by. I didn't know how this time-traveling crap worked. If I was given the opportunity to cheat the system, screw the consequences for the future, I would take it. Besides, for all his illiteracy and focus on food, Tony wasn't in terrible shape. If that same woman came at me again and he wasn't completely intoxicated, I might have a chance at taking her down. I guess we'd just have to wait and see if the opportunity presented itself.

By the time I walked out of the library, clutching a stack of papers in both arms, I realized poor Tony was pretty famished. I had gotten so distracted by everything that had happened this morning that I had forgotten to eat breakfast. And now that I remembered it, I couldn't stop thinking about it. It was like there was a gaping black hole in my stomach, one that was eating me from the inside out. I needed food. *Now.*

"So this is what it's like being a college-aged guy." I chuckled to myself as I walked back to the truck. "Constant starvation."

Once I reached the vehicle, I shifted my papers to one arm and checked Tony's pockets for his car keys. Nothing. I had left them inside. Tony muttered a few choice expletives before flinging open the car door and striding back into the library. The lady sitting in front of the computer was old, probably late seventies. Her eyes, stationed behind a wiry pair of spectacles, reflected blue in the synthetic light of a computer screen. It seemed like she came right out of central casting for librarians. She lifted her gaze to me as I approached, glancing me up and down as a frown plagued her lips. She was probably thinking what I had first thought when I saw Tony: *what a schmuck.* Before I had a chance to open my mouth, she spoke in a frail, low voice that barely reached my ears.

"Did you leave your keys, honey?"

I expected some amount of resistance from Tony—"honey" not being a preferred title of his—but he surprised me by giving her a genuine smile. "Yes. Do you have them?"

The woman slowly pulled open a desk drawer and rifled in it for several seconds before carefully withdrawing the key ring. "Some nice lady returned them for you. St. Anthony must be smiling down on you today."

Tony paused. "St. Anthony?"

"Why, he's the patron saint of lost things."

"Oh," he replied, unsure of how to respond. "Well, tell him I said thanks."

As he took the keys from the desk, the woman smiled. "What a nice young man you are. There should be more young men like you." Even though her comment went against everything I had seen from Tony during the last few hours, I couldn't help but agree with her. He had actually shown some politeness and respect during the interaction that I hadn't seen him display before. Maybe Tony wasn't the complete blockhead I thought he was.

The second time around, I unlocked and started the truck without issue. I stepped back to let Tony drive and watched as he pulled out of the parking lot to head home. I couldn't help but be tense, and I had to fight the urge to make him check over his shoulder every few seconds. As we passed a Burger King, Tony began to turn in to stop for food, but I took control of the wheel and steered him back onto the main road. We were heading home. There was plenty to eat there. We didn't need to stop anywhere. He gave me a lot of crap about it, but I eventually overpowered him. If nothing else, during my time in his mind, I would teach him some self-control.

Tony had the radio tuned to alternative rock, but it didn't take long to find something that was more my style. Once Janis Joplin was blaring through the speakers, I instantly felt more at ease. Nothing had happened yet. There was still a chance I could be wrong about the whole Tony-abduction thing. There was nothing to say for sure that it was going to happen. Maybe I was wrong.

Tony drove for several minutes without noticing it. When he did, he didn't think anything of it. The glance in my rearview mirror wasn't enough to make out all the details. But the quick look at it did stir something in my subconscious, for I immediately felt an overwhelming sense of dread. Unsure of where this feeling was stemming from, I stepped forward in Tony's mind and squinted at the rearview mirror again. That's when I saw it, *really* saw it. There was a red minivan driving behind me with tinted windows. And it wasn't just any red minivan.

It was *the* red minivan.

I gasped, instinctively pressing on the brakes as my heart began to pound. The van slowed down and stayed close behind, maintaining an uncomfortably close distance that I hadn't noticed it was doing until now.

"Oh shit." I breathed, narrowing my eyes at the car, straining to see inside the windshield. The window was completely blacked out, obscuring the details of the person sitting behind the wheel. I could only just manage to make out their silhouette.

Feeding off my roiling fear, I felt Tony grow anxious, even though he wasn't completely sure why. I tried to calm both him and myself down by explaining that I didn't know for sure this was the same van. A quick glance in the rearview mirror that may or may not line up with my drunken memories from the night Eliza was taken didn't confirm anything. I needed to think logically. First off, did I know for sure the van behind me was the same van from the party? I needed to be sure before I started doing anything rash. Luckily, I was driving on a flat, straight road and could afford to glance back every few seconds. I tried to match it to the memory I had of the first vehicle. From what I could tell, it matched. Besides, how many cars were driving around Ohio with blacked-out windows? There couldn't be that many.

Second, was I sure the van was following me? At the moment, there was still a chance it was just a coincidence. They might've pulled onto the same road as me and could be driving along with no idea I thought they were following me. There was only one way to know. Using a trick I learned from one of the countless cop shows I binged off Netflix, I pulled off the main road onto a side road. Following the road as far as I could, I made a right and followed that road back to the main one I had originally been driving on. I was purposefully driving in a full circle. Once we had completed the loop, I glanced behind me again. The minivan had stayed on me the whole time.

There was no reason for them to be driving around in circles—they were following me. The realization sent a chill racing down my spine. My head cleared with a sudden burst of adrenaline. I pulled to a stop in front of a red light at an intersection, shaking hands on the steering wheel with a white-knuckled grip.

The third thing to decide was what to do with this information.

Obviously, the most straightforward decision would be to go to the police. Even though I didn't know exactly what to say, I was pretty sure getting followed would count as suspicious behavior. But as soon as I brought up the idea of heading toward the station, Tony immediately shut it down. He had no intention of going to the police. I tried to convince him that this was dangerous, that he was being followed, and that we needed to get away. Apparently, this got jumbled in translation, and all he understood was "needed to get away," for next thing I knew, I was shoved to the back of his mind. Tony revved the engine, a grin spreading across his face. *What are you doing?* I asked him silently. His answer came swiftly: *car chase.*

Apparently Tony was a big fan of the *Fast and Furious* movies and had been meaning to test his driving skills for some time. And this seemed like the perfect opportunity. Much as I tried to convince him otherwise, he had already got it stuck in his mind. I guess this was happening.

Tony's eyes scanned the road before him, forming a plan.

Then without giving another moment for second-guessing, Tony slammed his foot on the gas.

The truck shot out in the middle of the street, swerving into oncoming traffic. Car horns erupted around us, but Tony ignored them and turned off into the rightmost lane. Flicking his eyes toward my rearview mirror, Tony saw the red minivan follow his trail. *So they want to play,* Tony thought. *All right. I can play.*

Tony shoved the gas pedal to the floor, weaving in and out of cars. His mind flashed back to the defensive driver's course his mom had first made him take when he got his license, although I was pretty sure this wasn't what she had in mind when she signed him up. Tires screeched as he made a sharp right onto a rural road. He glanced behind to see the other van do the same, choking black smoke trailing after its tires.

The minutes that followed passed in a blur of red stoplights and the scent of burned rubber. After the first few turns, I completely lost all sense of direction. I wasn't even sure if we were in the same town. But Tony seemed to think this was all great fun.

Without warning, the red minivan peeled away from us. Tony glanced around, eyes flicking from road to road as we passed, waiting for it to reappear, but it never did. When he was sure that we were alone, Tony let out a whoop, pumping a fist into the air. I breathed a sigh of relief from the back of his mind. And Tony was safe, for now. Finally, he let me step forward, and I slowed us down to something close to the speed limit. I couldn't wipe the smile off my face as we cruised down the now-empty highway. We had won this battle. I had beaten whatever system I was playing against.

Or so I thought. The road wasn't exactly empty. There was one car coming up quickly behind me. It was a black car, with one important word painted on its side. Once I saw the red and blue flashing lights, I suddenly understood why my pursuer had fled so abruptly.

"Awh shit," Tony muttered as he twisted the wheel toward the side of the road. "Shit, shit, *shit.*"

The police officer gave me two tickets, one for speeding and another for reckless driving. Tony tried to explain that someone had been following him, but understandably, the officer thought Tony was just trying to make up an excuse for burning rubber with friends.

Either way, the chase ended in the most anti-climactic way possible: with the victor driving home slowly with hunched shoulders and two infuriating pieces of paper crumpled in the cup holder.

III

"YOU WANT TO explain this?"

When I first opened the front door to see Mrs. Giordano, she looked almost exactly like I pictured her. Her brown eyes, angled with crow's feet, stared at Tony with a knowing glare. The dark hair surrounding her face was wiry and stuck out in all directions. Even from where I stood, I could smell the scent of cooking oil coming off her in waves.

In one olive-skinned hand, she clutched a bag of marijuana.

Tony caught sight of it and instantly his whole demeanor changed, day having gone from bad to way worse. "What the hell?" he cried, taking a step toward his mother. "You went into my room?"

"Of course, I did! I was going in to clean. It smelled like *merda* in there!" Tony instantly reversed and stepped back toward the door when Mrs. Giordano jumped to her feet, striding toward him with the bag outstretched. "You stupid boy, why are you bringing drugs into my good home? I'm calling the cops, and then I'm calling your father. Just wait till you see what they're going to do to you—"

"Jesus, Mom, calm down!" Tony held out both hands in a gesture of peace, but his mother was having none of it. I could see the fire in her eyes. Unlike the shouting of this morning, her voice was softer now, but the tone was edged and biting. Even though I didn't really know what was going on, I knew one thing for sure: Tony had screwed up big time. I stepped back in his mind, letting him take control. There was no way I was saving his ass this time. This was his screw up. Now, it was time to sit back and watch the show.

"Where did you get this?" hissed Mrs. Giordano.

"Mom, it's not—"

"where did you get this?"

Tony swallowed, trying to pull together a coherent thought. As he stared into his mother's dirt-brown eyes, I read his every thought. He knew exactly whose bag it was. And surprisingly, the excuse he gave next was the God's honest truth. "I swear, Ma," Tony began, "it's not mine. It's my friend Benny's. You know Benny, right?"

His mother's furious breathing stilled. "That small boy from two blocks over?"

"Yes." He breathed, relieved she made the connection. "Yes, that Benny."

"What about him?"

"Well, you know, I've been telling you Benny's having a rough time—with the divorce and everything—and he knew that if his dad found weed in his room, he'd kill him. He's really not in a good spot right now, and he needed someone to hold it for him, just for a couple days before he could find someplace to keep it permanently. I was doing him a favor, Ma."

I watched Mrs. Giordano weigh his story, gaze flicking from her son to the weed in her hand. "Are you lying to me, *figlio*?"

"No, Ma, I'm not."

She studied his face, his eyes, searching for a chink in his armor. And when she found none, her anger instantly dissolved. "Oh, *mio amore*!" she shouted, throwing her arms around her son. "You gave me such a scare! I knew my boy wasn't doing drugs." She pulled back, reaching up one hand to pinch his right cheek. "My good boy would never do such a thing. But—" She swung the baggie up and smacked Tony's face, hard. He yelped, rubbing it as she continued, "*Sei un idiota!* Don't you ever bring drugs into my good home again! You give that bag right back to that poor boy tonight, and I never want to see it again. Is that understood?"

"Yes, Ma," Tony muttered, still massaging his reddened cheek.

"And what are these?" Mrs. Giordano stepped forward to take the stack of papers from Tony's hands.

The speeding tickets. With a smoothness I didn't think Tony was capable of, he slipped the tickets into his back pocket with one hand and passed the pile of papers to his mother with the other. "See?" he said, a hint of pride in his voice. "I really was doing homework."

"Oh, my sweet *polpetta*! You are such a good boy!"

Mrs. Giordano continued to fawn over Tony for some time, all second thoughts about his behavior completely forgotten. As the conversation length went from long to interminable, he began inching his way toward the stairs. His mother called after him, "I'm making a big ziti dinner, so stay home tonight, you hear me?"

"Okay, Ma," Tony replied, stepping carefully up the stairs. He breathed a sigh of relief when he made it to the doorway of his bedroom. Mrs. Giordano was still talking to herself in a mix of English and Italian when Tony closed the door. He had had the foresight to grab the bag of marijuana when his mother was distracted, and he held it up now along with the parking tickets. I was slightly impressed in the way he was able to get himself out of that one. I was almost getting worried for him (it wasn't like I enjoyed watching someone get chastised by their mother) but he knew exactly what to say to calm her down.

As I took back control and spun around to face the room, though, I realized she was right. It did smell nasty in there, and it wasn't just dirty laundry. I followed the putrid odor, walking to Tony's bed. Crouching down, I pulled up the bed skirt to reveal a bowl of milk and Cheerios. The milk had obviously gone bad, and I suppressed a gag as I pulled out it out. "Ew, Tony," I muttered, breathing only through my mouth. "Gross." *How did I not smell that this morning?* I was probably too frazzled by the waking-up-as-a-guy thing to notice. But as I pulled it out, something behind it caught my eye. Reaching out, I plucked another smaller bag of weed from between two shoeboxes. As Tony's mind made the connection, I couldn't help but laugh.

Tony hadn't lied. What Mrs. Giordano had found was Benny's bag of weed. What she *hadn't* found was Tony's personal stash of weed, which I had just accidently discovered. "You son of a bitch." I chuckled, rolling my eyes. "I can't believe you." Satisfied that his own stash hadn't been raided, Tony stepped forward. He carefully picked up the two bags and moved them to a new hiding spot, behind his high school graduation picture frame.

As Tony straightened the frame out, elated at his success in outsmarting his mother, I heard a rumbling growl. Oh crap. With the excitement of when Tony had first walked in the front door, we had both forgotten to grab something to eat in the kitchen. If he was hungry before, now he was absolutely starving. This was apparently not as uncommon an occurrence as I would've thought, Tony had a secret stash of food in his room that he was more than happy to break into.

While Tony began devouring Doritos by the handful, I started looking over the articles again. The problem was I didn't know what I was searching for. A part of me hoped that if I just read the lines over and over and over again, something would click and everything would become clear. But it didn't. As far as I could tell, there was nothing in common between Eliza and Tony besides the mysterious discovery of the toys. But there had to be some connection, some rhyme or reason in all this. I just couldn't find it.

I eventually let out a groan of frustration and stood, stretching my arms above my head. This was wasting my time. Besides, Tony was bored out of his mind. I needed to do something to get him up and moving. As I forced him to put down his third bag of Cheetos, I remembered the self-defense moves I had printed out at the library. That was perfect, something to keep him occupied that was actually useful. I leafed through the papers, scanning the different moves and techniques. Tony could totally figure this out. I grabbed his phone and pulled up YouTube, searching for a good playlist to start with. I eventually landed on a '60s–'80s playlist that opened with AC/DC's "T.N.T." Perfect. I nodded to the strong rhythm and placed the papers down, moving to the back of Tony's mind and hoping he got the hint. He immediately picked up on it, throwing a right hook at his invisible attacker. He shifted his weight from foot to foot, the movement natural from all the boxing he had watched over the years. Once again, I was surprised by what Tony could do when he put his mind to things.

As the minutes wore on and Tony downed his enemy again and again (his subconscious told me he was picturing Drago from *Rocky IV* as his invisible foe), my mind kept coming back to that red van. At the moment, that was the only tangible evidence I had connecting Tony and Eliza together. There had to be something more there, something I could use to figure out who was causing this. If only I could see the driver clearly…

A knock on the door pulled my distracted mind back to the present. Tony was coated in a thin sheen of sweat and breathing hard. Dare I say he was actually having fun?

"What?" he called out, wiping his forehead with the back of his right hand.

The familiar voice came in response. "I'm leaving with Jacqueline to get some more ricotta!" shouted Tony's mother. "When I get home, I expect those drugs to be gone! Do you understand?"

"Yes, Mom!" Tony shouted back with no intention of following through.

"Oh, that's my good boy!" I heard Mrs. Giordano retreat down the steps, calling out to Jackie in Italian. Now that Tony had stopped, the exercise lost its momentum and a wave of exhaustion swept over him. It came to my attention that he had done more in this single morning than he had probably done in the entirety of the past month. I couldn't even fault him for being tired. After making him change once again out of his sweaty clothes and into something cleaner, he shoved the papers off the covers of his bed and collapsed onto the mattress. He closed his eyes, and moments later, he was out.

I could tell that not too much time had passed when next he woke. It was still the same day, still afternoon. Granted, more like late afternoon, but I hadn't lost too much of the day. I watched Tony roll over, ready to go back to sleep. I was about to force him out of bed when he caught a whiff of something that instantly sent a burst of wakefulness into his mind. But this time, unlike the sour milk incident, the smell was good. There was something in his room, something baked.

Tony sat up quickly, scanning the room for the source. It took mere seconds for him to spot the tinfoil covered tray sitting on his dresser. Peeling back the foil, he peered at the cookies underneath. They smelled *amazing*. I could sense the Cheetos and Doritos from before hadn't really done it for Tony. I tried to insert some sort of self-control, but even I couldn't override the furious, unstoppable appetite that overtook him.

As he shoveled in the first cookie, he barely processed the warm sugar and chocolate as it melted in his mouth. These were definitely homemade. While Tony continued shoving cookies into the black hole that was his stomach with one hand, I pulled his laptop over to me with the other and opened a tab for Google. This freaking minivan was bothering me. Maybe if I could figure out exactly what kind of van it was, I would be able to identify where I knew it from.

The minutes wore on as I scrolled through page after page and consumed cookie after cookie. Much as I tried, I couldn't find an exact match. And while I was in the chase, I hadn't thought to check the make of the car. I couldn't help feeling that these stupid mistakes were eventually going to catch up to me. Tony was on his eighth cookie when he yawned. "C'mon, Tony," I muttered, clicking past photo after photo. "Don't give me that crap. You just slept." None of these cars exactly fit what I had seen, but then again, this was really like looking for a needle in a haystack. I stifled another yawn. *What the hell?* He really shouldn't be this tired. Maybe the workout was more intense than I thought.

My head was really heavy. It tilted forward, slowly dropping into my lap before I yanked it back up. My eyes began to flutter shut, but I forced them open. I felt a thick fog surround my mind as the edges of my vision blurred.

What was going on? This wave of exhaustion came from out of nowhere. It was almost like I was…

My tired eyes caught the cookie still clutched in my hand.

"What the f…" I breathed, the last word dissipating as my eyes closed. My head fell forward into the laptop, and I felt the keys pressing into my forehead.

My eyes fluttered open one last time to see the door creak open.

Everything went black.

IV

WHEN I REGAINED consciousness, I had the now-familiar sensation of waking up in a different place from when I fell asleep. I felt the sun rays through my eyelids, signaling the new day, but I squeezed them shut in anger.

Are you serious, Tony? He couldn't have just eaten one or two cookies like any normal person, he had to eat nearly a *dozen*. And the cookies just happened to be drugged. What a perfect end to that whole experience. My annoyance shifted to anger and then dulled to desperation. That entire day was wasted. All I had done was drive to the library and back, practice some self-defense moves, sleep, and eat crap. None of it had done any good. Now I was in another body, and I had still learned *nothing.*

I was cursed—cursed to relive all these abductions, cursed to know all the answers, and cursed with the fact that I could do nothing about it. I was at the front of it all, but I was powerless to stop it.

"Shit!" I screamed, the frustration and fear bottled within

me all releasing in one word. As soon as I did, my eyes shot open.

Wait a minute. I know that voice.

My eyes moved around the room, scanning. I didn't recognize the television show posters on the walls or the lava lamp in the corner. But when I sniffed the air, I instantly recalled what scent tinged the air: *lavender. Who am I?* There was a phone lying on the yellow-carpeted floor, plugged into a nearby outlet. I reached for it and held the home button.

"What day is today?" I asked softly. The voice was airy and timid, distinctly feminine.

"It's Wednesday, February 27." A little under a month had passed since Tony. That wasn't so bad.

"What's my name?"

It thought for a moment before replying, *"Your name is Jackie Giordano."*

"Wait, what?" Leaping up, I raced to the other side of the room and skidded to a stop in front of the dresser. Sure enough, the mirror in front of me reflected the petite olive-skinned form of Tony's sister. I wove the fingers of both hands together, placing them behind my head as I absorbed the image in front of me.

Once I was sure of what I was seeing, I repeated, "Shit."

PART THREE

Jacqueline

I

WHEN ELIZA WENT missing, nothing was the same. Everything felt off, as if the world had shifted slightly off its axis. Eliza's earth was lighthearted, fun, and balanced. With her gone, it felt like she took a piece of life with her. It was impossible to get comfortable in a room when even the smallest things had the possibility of drawing forth her memory. There were certain places I couldn't go anymore: the nearby mall, our favorite nail salon, the coffee shop across the high school. Her memory was imprinted on those locations. It was too painful going there without her by my side. If I had no choice but to go to those places, I tried to ignore the feeling, but then I felt like I was ignoring her, which just made things worse.

The fact was that when Eliza left, everything changed. And when I opened the door to Jackie's bedroom, I expected to feel something similar. If I remembered correctly, I had woken up in Tony's body on February 12. If today was February 27, that meant Tony had been missing for several weeks. Things in the Giordanos' house should feel different. But no. I could hear Mrs. Giordano in the kitchen, bustling around and chatting with someone in Italian. Her tone was calm, and I could hear laughter mixing with her words. There was a television on, playing some news network. If I didn't know better, I wouldn't have suspected anything was amiss, let alone a missing person.

"I have to figure out what's going on," I muttered, throwing the door open the rest of the way and making my way down the steps. As I turned the corner in the kitchen, I saw Mrs. Giordano standing over the kitchen table. She had a rosary in one hand and a Bible in the other, carefully placing them in a leather purse in front of her. Across from the kitchen was another room, a lounge area that held a small television and a rounded couch. A middle-aged man with a sharp Italian face and dark eyes was seated on the couch, his gaze fixed to the screen. He looked up when I entered the room and smiled. *"Figlia,"* he cooed, ushering me toward him. "How are you?"

"Good," Jackie answered on autopilot. She strode to him, leaning over to allow him to place a kiss on her cheek before straightening. That's when I took over. "Papa, where's Tony?"

He crinkled his brow at me. "What do you mean, where's Tony?"

"Where is he?"

"You know I don't know."

"But—"

Mrs. Giordano, who apparently hadn't noticed me enter the room, cut me off with a cry of "Jacqueline, you're up! I'm so glad I get to see you before I go." She walked to me, planting a wet kiss on my opposite cheek.

I spun to face her. "Where's Tony?"

Making an expression identical to her husband's, her

eyebrows knit together as her eyes narrowed. "How should I know? He said he was staying with his friends somewhere. With that Benny kid, no doubt. Oh, I knew he was bad news."

He said he was with his friends? I never said that when I was Tony. But upon searching Jackie's memories, I found that he had left a scribbled note on his desk saying that he was taking some time off from school to relax with his friends. They had tried calling his phone, but it was either off or dead, as the call went right to voice mail.

I knew that Tony hadn't written that note because *I* hadn't written that note. That could only mean that someone had forged it. Whoever took Tony had planned ahead. They were getting smarter about things now. With Eliza, they had just taken her out of the blue, leaving room for an investigation and prying eyes. With Tony, though, they had been smart enough to lay a contingency plan.

The reality of the situation slowly washed over me, and I could hardly believe it. "You're not looking for him." I breathed.

"Why should we? He'll come back when he's ready." Mr. Giordano turned to face me from his position on the couch. He must have seen something behind my eyes, for he added, "Why? Do you know where he is?"

"Is he in trouble?" interjected Mrs. Giordano. I could hear the slightest hint of fear sharpening her words.

To be completely honest, I had no idea where Tony was. I was pretty sure he wasn't hanging out with his buddies, but I had no proof he was in actual danger. How could I even begin to explain all this? And even if I tried to, what could the Giordanos do? They could call the police, but that had obviously proved useless in Eliza's case. Besides, there was no reason for Jackie to suspect something was wrong. If I wasn't living inside her head, she wouldn't have any suspicion that her brother was in danger. So how could I realistically bring up the possibility?

"No," I finally whispered, eyes focused on Jackie's navy blue socks. "I mean, I don't think so. I just wish I knew where he was."

Mrs. Giordano threw her arms up, blowing out a sigh of annoyance. "That *bambino ingrato*! Upsetting his whole family." She wagged a finger at me, giving off the impression that I was the one whom she was peeved at. "When he gets back, he'll wish he stayed away longer."

I nodded by way of agreement, not trusting myself to say another word. Mrs. Giordano turned away, muttering to herself, and I heard the front door close behind her. I was about to step away when I felt a tug on my sleeve.

"It's okay, *miele*," Mr. Giordano said, giving me a sad smile. "He'll come home when he's ready."

I nodded again, and I couldn't tell if the budding tears were mine or Jackie's. "Thanks, Papa."

By the time I made it back to Jackie's bedroom, my mind had cleared considerably. I couldn't dwell on what had been done. I could only prepare for what was to come. There was nothing substantial for me to work with for Tony's "case." Unlike Eliza, I didn't have articles to look at or police reports to pick apart. But I did have one thing in Tony's case that I didn't have in Eliza's: access to a crime scene. His bedroom was right next to Jackie's. If I did some searching, maybe I could find something that would lead me closer to who was behind this. In some of those crazy smart cop shows, they could find a button from a jacket and deduce all sorts of things about the person who had committed the crime. Who was to say I couldn't do the same?

As I began mustering the courage to walk into Tony's room, Jackie suddenly reminded me that she had college classes to go to. Crap. I had forgotten that school was a thing. The first thought I had was to ditch for the day, but then I thought again. Jackie was going to be taken soon, maybe even today. Obviously, staying home from school had not worked for Eliza or Tony. Hopefully, going to school with security cameras at every corner and hundreds of students milling about would be enough to deter whoever was doing this. They obviously weren't afraid to break into someone's home, but maybe they would be more wary of doing something in public. All the previous abductions had been private, so forcing whoever was doing this out into the open would put them out of their comfort zone.

Still, I would at least need an hour or two to sort through Tony's room and see what I could find. Thinking quickly, I strode to my bedroom door and flung it open, calling out, "Papa?"

"Yes, *miele*?" came the shouted reply.

"My morning class was canceled, so I'm going to head out a little later than normal. My next class starts at eleven."

There was a pause. "Okay! Don't be late!"

"I won't!" Breathing a sigh of relief, I mentally told Jackie to get changed out of her pajamas, which were really just a loose long-sleeve shirt from high school and baggy sweatpants. Once she had gotten into a faded Captain America hoodie and tattered jeans (the girl had good taste), I strode into Tony's room. Jackie's subconscious reminded me about makeup, but I ignored her. We could forgo getting caked in foundation and blush for a day. When Jackie tried to argue with me, I convinced her there were more important things to worry about. She put up a daring fight but eventually backed down.

When I pushed open the door to Tony's room, I expected to see objects out of place, maybe an overturned chair or something to insinuate there had been some sort of struggle. But much to my surprise, the room looked exactly the same. There were no out-turned drawers, spilled drinks, or shifted furniture. In essence, nothing to signal there had been any sort of trouble. There were some spots of disorganization—the dirty laundry clothes piled in the bottom of the closet, a spread of wrappers around the garbage can from missed "Kobe" shots—but all that was there before he was taken. Then again, Tony was out cold when he was (I assumed) dragged away. As I continued looking around, I didn't even spot a crumb from those freaking cookies. Damn, whoever was behind this cleaned up good. I ran my finger over the table top, and it came away coated in gray film. The thin layer of dust cloaking the room made me suspect that Mrs. Giordano hadn't bothered cleaning while Tony was away since she assumed he was coming back. So all the cleanup was done the same night he was taken.

The woman must have taken his phone because it wasn't in the room. I even tried calling it from Jackie's cell, but it still went right to voice mail. It was probably turned off, shoved into the glove compartment of that stupid van. The one thing she didn't take, though, was Tony's laptop. It was sitting closed on his bed, in the exact location where I last left it. The computer was pretty heavy and clunky, so I supposed whoever took Tony didn't want to bother dragging it downstairs too. That worked in my favor because it gave me an opportunity to search for any clues.

I flipped the laptop open, only to be met with a locked screen. Not a problem. I could just use Tony's memory. But I quickly realized that I wasn't in Tony's head anymore, and Jackie had no idea what the password was for her brother's computer. "Ugh," I groaned. This was going to be harder than I thought. Shutting my eyes, I began searching Jackie's memories for any clues as to what it could be. I quickly came to the conclusion that she knew very little about her brother and what he spent his time on. I tried his and Jackie's birthday (June 7) with no success. I tried the usuals: *password, 123456, qwerty.* Still nothing. Annoyance setting in, I sat back in the chair and started to scan the room. There had to be something here to work with. I looked over his sparse collection of comics, a Newton's cradle, and dusty high school yearbooks. He was a generic college student with no particular interests or talents. His password could've been literally anything.

"God, Tony," I muttered. "Why do you have to be so bland?" And why couldn't I have been smart enough to access Tony's passwords when I was living inside his head? I was beginning to give up hope when I saw it. A poster, centered right above his desk. It was from a Marvel movie, *Avengers: Infinity War.* I liked to think of myself as a superhero movie connoisseur, having seen nearly all in current existence. There was even one time I won a superhero trivia competition on a cruise. Finally, all that seemingly useless knowledge was about to come in handy. I tried to think back to all the movies I had seen. Was there anything in them that could be used as a password—something about one of the heroes, a catchphrase, inside joke, anything that stood out? There was that one

Wi-Fi password from *Dr. Strange*, but I think that was too out there, kind of hard to remember. Even so, I tried it anyway. No luck. Wait, I did remember something, from one of those *Iron Man* movies I was watching when I was Eliza. One of the characters had used a special code to protect their computer system. It wasn't Iron Man's password, but his friend that had another robot suit. What was it exactly? I thought about it for a second. Then carefully, I typed it letter by letter.

I couldn't control my surprised laughter when the computer unlocked. Wow. That was kinda cool. Maybe Tony wasn't as lame as I first thought. But I didn't have time to dwell on his idiosyncrasies. I had business to attend to. The first thing I checked was his school e-mail. It was clogged with messages from students and teachers alike.

Dude, you weren't in class again today. That group project isn't going to do itself…

Mr. Giordano, your essay is two weeks late…

bro, why r u not answering ur phone? u dead or something?…

I cringed, that last response hitting a little too close to what feared might be the truth. They had no idea that Tony had way more important things to worry about than late assignments or group projects. After skimming through every e-mail since the night of his disappearance, I couldn't find anything suspicious apart from a few exchanges regarding a stolen answer key for the biology final. But it sounded like the whole escapade fell through, so even that was a dead-end.

After an hour or so had passed, I closed the laptop in defeat. There were no leads to anything useful. I figured Tony's laptop would be my best bet at finding something, so now I was onto plan B: searching Tony's room by hand. I walked to stand in the doorway, then spun around so I was facing the room. Stepping forward carefully, I tried to follow a path I thought the abductor might've followed in order to take Tony. My eyes scanned the surroundings, comparing what I was looking at to what I remembered seeing, carefully checking for anything out of place. From what I could tell, everything was as it had been. Maybe they shoved something under his bed, trying to hide it. On my knees, I peered under the bed, turning on the flashlight on Jackie's phone for a better view. When it was clear there wasn't anything, I lifted my head and sat back on my heels. That's when I saw it.

It was subtle, so subtle that I almost didn't see it at first, even against the off-white carpet. If I wasn't sitting eye level with it, I probably wouldn't have noticed it. The line of what appeared to be dirt stretched for about a foot, from the corner of the bed out toward the door frame. I rose to my feet, keeping my eyes fixed on the mark. Now that I knew what to look for, I couldn't keep my eyes off the discoloration. Although it was long, it wasn't wide. From my point of view, I guess it was about six inches across. It almost looked like the shape of…

"A footprint," I breathed, setting my foot alongside it. The smear was almost identical, as if someone dragged their foot along the carpet on their way to the door

Closing my eyes, I tried to picture it in my head, like some sort of sicko horror movie. Tony collapsed in bed, head mashing the keyboard of his laptop. The door slowly opened, revealing a figure standing on the threshold. They took a tentative step forward, testing to see if he was completely out. Once they were sure, they moved quickly. Grabbing him by his feet, they pulled him off the bed, and he fell, dead-weight, to the floor. As they dragged him toward the door, their feet scraped against the threaded carpet. It only took a minute, maybe two, to move Tony over the threshold. There was no one in the house to witness it or report it. And the only person who could've stopped it moved into a new body the moment he lost consciousness.

A shiver rolled down my spine. I needed to save Eliza. But not just Eliza. I realized now this was so much bigger than just my friend. I needed to save Tony and possibly Jackie too. Although I couldn't stop these abductions from happening, I could try to figure out who was behind all this. I was given all the pieces.

I just needed to solve the puzzle fast enough.

11

I SPENT THE next few minutes doing another sweep but didn't find anything else amiss. When I was completely sure I hadn't missed anything, I glanced at my watch. It was nearly ten. Jackie's second class was going to start in a little over an hour, and if I didn't leave soon, I was going to be late. I left Tony's room feeling slightly more confident. The footprint was proof that *something* had happened and that whoever was doing this made mistakes. They weren't infallible. Maybe going to the college would be enough to deter whoever was behind this for at least a day or two. As I considered it, though, the thought of my going to college sent a spike of nervousness through me. The *real* Vanessa was only a junior in high school. I hadn't even started my college apps yet. The thought of attending college classes seemed almost as scary as getting abducted. Keyword: almost.

Swallowing my inhibitions, I followed Jackie's lead back to her room and picked up her backpack from where she had left it, leaning against her bed. She made sure her cellphone and license were snug inside her back pocket before hurrying down the stairs.

"Bye, Papa!" Jackie called as she plucked a set of car keys off the hook beside the front door. I heard him respond in casual Italian, which Jackie mentally translated to "Have a nice day, honey." As soon as I stepped out the door, my eyes saw what was in the driveway. Or rather, what *wasn't* in the driveway. The only car there was the Giordano family car. The idol of masculinity, Tony's prized vehicle, was nowhere in sight. At first, I was confused. Jackie's subconscious informed me that the family had assumed he had taken it when he "went off with his friends." But as I thought about it, I realized what really happened.

"That bitch," I laughed mirthlessly. "She stole his truck." Before she dragged Tony out of his room, she must have swiped his keys off the dresser. It was the last step of the woman's plan: to take Tony's car, the final proof that he really was away with friends. Jackie's subconscious told me she was slightly disappointed because she liked to steal Tony's truck when he slept in and drive it around town. Recently, he had taken to hiding his keys from her to make them more difficult to find, but he must have forgotten about it when he was stuffing his face with cookies.

That left our only option: the family car. It was a Chevy, dark green on worn wheels that might've once been new before it went through years of use. The front license plate was missing a few screws, causing it hang at a precarious angle. The passenger side mirror was completely missing, which I was pretty sure was illegal to drive without. As I moved closer, I saw something flashing in the light on one of the wipers. At first, I just thought there was a crack in the mirror that was refracting light back into my eyes.

It all happened in a fraction of a moment. One second, I was staring at the small object under the rightmost wiper blade. Then I blinked. The faded pinwheel came into focus.

And the world stopped spinning.

*

I'm very, very small. I feel the rumbling of the seat beneath me, the gentle swaying of the car. There's a red pinwheel in my left hand. I giggle, blowing a puff of air into the toy and watching it spin.

"Okay," Mommy says. "Let's play a game." My ears catch the last word, and I look toward her, sitting in the front seat.

"What game?" a blond girl to my left asks. She's my sister. "Is it 'I Spy'?"

"No," Mommy replies, keeping her eyes on the road. "It's called 'Duck.'"

"Like 'Duck Duck Goose'?"

"No. This is different. When I tell you to duck, you need to duck under the seat as quickly as you can and stay quiet and still."

Growing bored with the stream of words, I bring my focus back to my pinwheel. It isn't until Mommy starts saying the rules of the game that I start to listen again.

"It's fun because you're allowed to take off your seat belts." I let out a cheer and click the button to release the restraint. The belt slides back into the seat, and I step down onto the carpet below. Along with the blond girl on my left, there is a boy at my right with jet black hair. We all laugh and smile together, enjoying the unexpected freedom. A baby in a car seat beside me giggles too. She clutches a stuffed bear in one hand.

We play the game for a while, jumping up and down on command. After a few minutes, though, something happens. Flashing lights appear behind us, and instantly, all mirth vanishes from the car. The woman yells something I haven't heard before.

"Mommy," my sister says. "That's a bad word."

But Mommy isn't listening.

My sister says a few more things, but I'm not listening to her, either. I'm distracted by the colorful lights and my other sister's increasingly loud screams. A green sign races past the window, and I'm just able to read the sign with my broken knowledge of English: I-71.

When Mommy yells something again, I almost can't hear it over all the other noise.

"I can't control it!"

We all fall to the floor again. Loud bangs come from outside. Without warning, I'm thrown to the side of the car. My back slams against the window, head cracking against the glass. There's a loud crash, and I feel myself flying through the air.

I feel a terrible pain. I see black.

৵

My eyes shot open. I dragged air into my burning lungs as my equilibrium slowly returned. My heart threw itself against my ribcage, the tension still palpable in the air. It slowly became apparent that I was on the ground, pieces of gravel digging into my palms. I shook my head slowly, trying to absorb what just occurred.

Another flash of memory. But this one was much longer and more vivid than the others I'd experienced. More importantly, in this memory, there were several other children with me: two girls (one toddler and one baby) and a boy. The blond-haired girl and the boy weren't familiar, but I had seen that baby before, the one in the car seat…

My stomach flipped when I placed the face. I had seen the baby in the other vision when I was Eliza, the one with the teething toy. The child in that memory had given the toy to the baby, had called her "sister." These flashbacks weren't random—they were all connected. Maybe they were of the same family, a family with three sisters and a brother. There were parents too. In the vision with the toy car, I had seen a man, perhaps their father. And in the most recent vision, there was a woman that the other sister had called "Mommy." A whole family, trapped in the memories I was reliving.

I was done with questioning whether any of this was real. I was in too deep. It had to make the jump and say that it was real. Otherwise, I would drive myself insane with the constant questioning. But what did it all mean? As my mind ran through the events of the last few seconds again and again, I started to feel a tickle in the back of my mind, a connection somewhere, like something was clicking into place.

And then I realized…

Two girls, a guy, and me. Eliza, Jackie, Tony, and I. Eliza's blond hair matched, as well as Jackie and Tony's dark hair. The two children with dark hair seemed to be the same height and same age, almost like they were twins. I blinked in shock as it all came into clarity.

We were the four children.

III

MY MIND SPUN so fast I could barely keep up. The pieces that had seemed so random and difficult to fit together were falling into place quickly now, almost too quickly. I was having trouble following my own racing thoughts.

We were the four children in the car. But even though the connection had been made, it still left many unanswered questions. I didn't know if all these flashbacks were repressed memories of mine—or something else. If the other three children were Eliza, Tony, and Jackie, did that make me... *the baby*? Then why was I viewing the memories from the other children's point of view? Shouldn't I be viewing them from the baby's? Or was the baby someone completely different? Maybe there was another child that hadn't gone missing yet. Did that mean that after Jackie, I would be transferred into yet *another* body?

Even more mysterious than that was the woman who drove the car. The toddler thought of her as "Mommy." I was pretty sure I hadn't seen her before, in memory or otherwise, but what if I had? What if she was the woman that took Eliza? I didn't get a clear look at her face during the vision, only the back of her head. But she had a similar hair type. What if it was her? Who was she? And why was she hunting us down? If we were the children in the vision, did that make her our—

I blinked, halting that train of thought. No, she couldn't be our mother. There was no way. I had been with Eliza since she was a kid. There was no way she was adopted. She would have told me. As for Tony and Jackie, well, it *was* possible, I supposed. I hadn't known them long enough to really get to know them, so I guess they might've been adopted. I had only scratched the surface of Jackie's memories, and even though she didn't think she was adopted, maybe she was missing something she hadn't known to look for. There was only one way to find out if they were adopted, and that was to ask.

I forced my racing thoughts to slow to a crawl. I needed to focus on one question at a time. Otherwise, I would get completely overwhelmed by it all and I wouldn't be able to think clearly. Once I figured out if Jackie and Tony were adopted, then I would see how that information fit into everything else I had seen. And how the woman and the car fit in.

I rose to my feet, placing one foot beneath me at a time. There was a stinging pain in my left hand. I had been clutching the keys so hard they were cutting my palm. Sliding the key ring onto my pinkie, I did a back pivot and began to walk shakily back to the house. Even though the revelation I had just experienced seemed to have taken hours, in reality, only a few minutes had passed. I hadn't left for class yet, and Jackie's father was still home. That meant there was still time to test my hypothesis.

After I shut the front door behind me, I leaned my back against it and breathed deeply. I attempted to calm my mind, focus on acting like I wasn't on the verge of a mental breakdown.

When I opened my eyes, Mr. Giordano was standing in front of me, a concerned look on his face.

"Jacqueline?" he asked, worry etched in his tone and expression. He held a newspaper in one hand, pointer finger tucked into its pages to hold his place. "Are you okay? I thought you were going to class."

"I am going to class," I answered quickly. "It's just… I have a question."

"Oh." My answer seemed to dispel some of his concern. But that concern was quickly replaced with confusion. "What's your question?"

I took a breath, hoping I wasn't making a big mistake, then blurted, "Am I adopted?"

Mr. Giordano's eyes widened for a moment. "Of course not." His answer left no room for question. "Why would you think that, *mio amore*?"

Before I answered, I took a moment to study his face. His eyebrows were pushed together, not quite touching but almost. I could tell the muscles in his jaw was tight, his mouth pressed into a tight line. The expression read confusion, adamancy—and a little hurt. Each emotion was distinct and authentic. To the best of my ability, I couldn't find an indication that he was lying.

I finally met his gaze and felt a blossom of shame bloom in my chest. This was stupid. Neither Jacqueline nor he had done anything to deserve my placing them in this awkward situation. "I…" I trailed off, then replied with the first excuse I could think of. "My friend Meghan—she just found out she was adopted. She was really upset about it, and it just got me thinking. I just wanted to be sure, you know?" In real life, Vanessa's life, my friend Meghan's parents had told her she was adopted right before her twelfth birthday. Even though it was several years ago, I still remembered it clearly. It shook up our whole friend group pretty badly. It seemed slightly better to base the false excuse in fact, even if the truth wasn't from Jackie's life but my own.

Now, Mr. Giordano continued to stare at me, but the confusion had left his face. "Oh, *miele*," he sighed. "Of course you and your brother aren't adopted. In fact, you're a spitting image of your mother." He motioned over his shoulder, adding quickly, "If you need proof, I can get out your baby books."

I shook my head fervently. "No, Papa, it's fine. I didn't actually think I was adopted. I just—wanted to know for sure."

There was a pause before he replied, "Okay." He seemed apprehensive for a moment, but then he wrapped his arms around me. I mentally stepped back to allow Jackie to accept the embrace. "*Ti amo.*"

"*Ti amo, anch'io*," Jackie whispered back before pulling away.

When I finally made it back to the car and sat down in the driver's seat, I was pretty shaken. Because I hadn't thought all of that through, I had just upset Jackie's dad, who would probably tell Mrs. Giordano, which Jackie would probably hear about later tonight. It didn't make any sense for us to be related, even if the number and gender of the children from the vision aligned with the abductions. I was making assumptions, drawing conclusions that weren't based in any real fact. I made a vow that before I jumped to any more conclusions, I would make sure I had the proper information to back it up.

So if they hadn't been adopted, then maybe I was wrong about the whole sibling connection. But I still couldn't shake the feeling that there was more to that vision than I had seen. The road sign flashed again in my head: I-71. The vision had ended in a crash. That meant that an accident had occurred on I-71. And because I knew the location of where the car crashed, I might be able to find an article or a report about it. News outlets reported major crashes, didn't they? *That* meant I could figure out who was in the car and hopefully find some real answers.

Shoving the keys into the ignition, I turned on the engine and glanced at the clock on the dashboard. Jackie's first class was starting in less than five minutes. "Oops," I muttered. "Guess we're missing that class too." Besides, I had work to do. I guess my college plan had to be put to the side for a while. Even so, I knew I couldn't stay at the house. I was pretty sure I had been able to convince Mr. Giordano with my explanation of the adoption question, but I was also pretty sure I wouldn't be able to explain my way out of a whole day of classes. So when I returned, I'd have to remember to pretend that I had gone to class as usual.

I twisted around to look out the back window. "Oh well, to Chuck E. Cheese it is."

IV

THE LIBRARY WAS slightly more crowded than when I had been there before, but the computers were still mostly empty. It was weird to think that just yesterday I had been here as Tony, but that yesterday had actually been weeks ago. Keeping up with this whole series of events was becoming more difficult than understanding the *X-Men* timeline. Luckily, unlike Tony, I didn't have to come up with some vague excuse about why he was actually studying. Jackie's subconscious told me that she came to the library regularly and actually enjoyed being around books. I sat across from a girl with statistics textbooks stacked around her. She seemed to be on the verge of a breakdown, and I gave her a sympathetic glance before plopping my backpack down beside me. The community college Jackie attended provided laptops to its students, so I was able to use hers instead of the library's.

Once the laptop booted up, I was able to start my search. I didn't have a lot to go on, but hopefully what I did have would be enough. First, I tried "car accident I-71." That turned out to be way too broad, drawing results from drunk drivers to car fires over a span of several years. I needed something more specific, like a time range. I thought back to the vision. From what I could recall, the child that was living in the vision could walk, talk, and read (sort of). So assuming that the child in the vision was around my age today, how long ago would she have been a toddler? Thinking quickly, I punched into the computer "youngest age baby can walk." The first link that came up a website was a forum for new moms, asking what a normal age for their child to start walking was. The consensus was between eight and eighteen months. Using that information, I could get a timeframe on when that vision occurred. Woah, I was hardcore Sherlocking this shit.

Well, I turned one in 2002. And the cars and signs that I spotted around the vehicle seemed pretty modern, so it was plausible that the memory occurred during that year. To check that theory, I typed "car accident I-71 2002." I scrolled through a few pages of results, but nothing matched. I tried the same for 2003, 2004, all the way up to the current year. Nothing. Then I tried counting down, going back from 2001. Even though the work was mind-numbingly boring, I wouldn't let myself move on until I was sure I had exhausted all possible options.

Finally, after nearly an hour of skimming article after article, I found one from 2000 titled "Shootout on I-71." Thinking back to the vision, the echo of loud popping rang in my ears. A shiver I didn't really understand rolled down my back. I clicked on the article and began to read.

ණ

> A sedan containing a woman and her four children was forced off of Highway I-71 Monday morning. The woman driving the vehicle, Nancy Harding, had fled her home after receiving notice that her children would be removed from her care by Child Protective Services on account of claims of mistreatment and mental instability. Harding left her home in her sedan with all four of her children inside, in an apparent attempt to deny CPS custody. Upon arriving at the scene and discovering Harding and the children gone, CPS called the local police. After several minutes of pursuit with no sign of the vehicle surrendering to arrest, the officers in pursuit made the decision to deploy a spike strip in advance of the fleeing sedan. With the wheels on Harding's vehicle rendered unusable, the car proceeded to swerve across several lanes of traffic, colliding with the median and making a full rotation before coming to rest. When an ambulance arrived on the scene, Harding and three of the children were found unconscious. The three children were not wearing seatbelts. All five were taken to the nearest hospital, and the children are now being treated in the ICU. We will be providing updates on their progress as information becomes available.

Nancy Harding. The name didn't hold any connection to me. But everything else I read matched up with what I had seen in the vision: the highway, the number of children, the police. Those loud bangs from the vision that I heard right before the car lost control must've been the tires popping when they rolled over the strip. And then the car crash. It all fit. But the article didn't state the names of the children. I scrolled to the bottom of the page, hoping for more information. There was another article listed as an update.

It was an obituary.

"Oh God," I whispered, horrified by the words but unable to look away. Three unnamed children, two girls and a boy. Died after injuries inflicted during a car accident. All siblings. I paused, narrowed my eyes at the text. *Three* of them had passed away. But there were four children in the article and in the vision. Did that mean that one child was still alive? Looking back at the obituary, the dates showed all the children who had died were two years old and above. That meant that only the youngest had survived. That must be the baby. But there was no way to check if my most recent hypothesis was correct, with the obituary being a dead-end with no other "recommended" links attached. And without an official age or name, there was no way for me to discover if the other child was alive.

Even so, the obituary confirmed that I was completely wrong about Eliza, Tony, Jackie, and I being connected to the four children. Three of them had died years ago, and the fourth was nowhere to be found. So I was back to square one with how all of them played into this. I still felt that we were somehow related to those four children, but there was nothing I could do at the moment to confirm or deny that theory. I had to wait until there was substantial evidence before I jumped to conclusions. I didn't want a repeat of what happened with Mr. Giordano.

Although what I found seemed to draw up more questions

than answers, I did acquire one sure thing: a name. Nancy Harding. Somehow, someway, Nancy Harding was involved in all this. I Googled her name, looking for anything that might be of use, and found that she had been charged for resisting arrest and ignoring a restraining order. So this wasn't the first time she had found herself in the crossfire of the law. There was a mugshot that I pulled up alongside the report. I stared at it, studying her face.

Nancy Harding had thick, wiry brown hair that stopped just before her shoulders. Her eyes were green, pensive, and determined. She had high cheekbones and a thin nose, the harsh light paling her skin to near white. But even with her back pressed to the black and white background and a numbered board clutched in both hands, she seemed almost… *normal.* Not how I would expect someone fleeing the police to look, or someone who had just lost three of their children. But according to the post, these photos were taken years ago. I tried again to match the face I saw on the screen to the one from Eliza's memory. She could've been the woman from Eliza's party, or maybe she wasn't. I just couldn't trust what I thought I remembered. The memory was too uncertain.

In the end, I decided that there were three new suspects for who this woman could be. She could be the mother from the article and the memory, Nancy Harding. That still didn't explain the motive, and none of the reasons I could come up with made sense. But I knew she was involved in this somehow, and that made her a suspect. My second theory was that the woman was the missing child, the baby who survived and hadn't appeared again in my research. The police report about the accident was from nearly twenty years ago. She must be a teen now, maybe older. Again, there was no reason for her to be going after us, but I couldn't completely disregard her. The third suspect for the woman was… *anyone*. There was always the possibility that the woman was someone I hadn't heard about yet and had no reason to suspect. That was what scared me the most: that I was searching for a pattern that wasn't there. That all this was completely random and none of my research would amount to anything concrete.

After everything I had discovered, I still had no definitive answers, only some random possibilities. But I definitely knew that Jackie was next on this woman's hit list since she found the toy. I needed a plan, some way that I could solve this before time ran out. Placing my head in my hands, I released a deep sigh.

How did I end up here? Police reports, abductions, a suspect list—this was all totally out of my league. Before all this, I was a teenager mourning and searching for my lost friend. Now I was trapped in some sort of sick mix of *Groundhog Day* and *Freaky Friday*, destined to relive the same mistakes over and over and over again, from other people's points of view. I shouldn't even be here, looking at this evidence in someone else's body. I had exhausted every idea I had. What I really needed was some advice, someone with an outside perspective on all this. But there was no one to talk to, no one to confide in. Everyone would think I was crazy. If only I could contact one of my friends, one of my family members, like Mom or Dad or…

Jeremy.

Jeremy, who always gave the best advice in all situations. Jeremy, who I regularly texted with. Jeremy, *who had mentioned my phone going missing when I had never lost it.* It had made no sense at the time, but when I was texting him about Mrs. Barrows, he mentioned me losing my phone. At first, I thought he was making a mistake, confusing me with someone else. But now, staring at Jackie's phone, I realized what must've happened.

I had never lost my phone. The *past* "me" had used it as an excuse to get advice from Jeremy when I was in someone else's body, when I was in Jackie's body. And this moment, in the library, was when I would "lose" my phone.

I had needed Jeremy's emergency assistance on more than one occasion, so over the years, I had memorized his number. Pulling out Jackie's phone, I punched in his number to call him. But then I paused. I wasn't in my own body, I was in Jackie's. That meant that my voice sounded different. Jeremy was smart, he would absolutely be able to tell if someone else picked up the phone pretending to be me. After thinking for a moment, I decided to text him.

> **Jackie:** hey Jeremy? It's Nessa. Lost my phone, using a friend's :/ i need some advice

There were only a few seconds of lapsed silence before I received a response.

> **Jeremy:** lol ur always losin things... like ur sanity :p

I couldn't help but smile and shake my head. Little did he know how much truth his snarky comment actually held.

> **Jackie:** haha very funny. can u actually help tho?
>
> **Jeremy:** yeah, wassup?

I used a few minutes to phrase my next words carefully. I needed to tell him just enough to understand but not too much to make him panic. I decided to spin a story, a story based in truth. That was the easiest way to get this out with the least questions asked.

Jackie: so i'm doing this narrative story thing for english, and i need some help on a scene. there's this girl, and she's getting chased by a woman. she knows that she's coming for her, but idk what i should have her do. hiding won't help, she'll find her eventually. thoughts?

This was right up Jeremy's ally. He loved creating stories and coming up with ideas for television shows and movies. I saw from the notifications that he looked at it for a few seconds before typing his response.

Jeremy: well in the survival guidebook, the two human reactions to conflict are fight or flight. so if she can't run or hide from it, i would have her stay and fight. Maybe instead of having the woman find her, the girl could find the woman. turn the tables, ya know?

I thought on that for a moment before replying.

Jackie: you mean like going out and searching for her?

Jeremy: yeah, why sit and wait? besides, i love strong characters... make her go after the woman herself

I sat there, reading the words again and again. Whoever was out for Jackie was going to find her—unless *I* went and found her first. I still remembered all those self-defense moves Tony had worked on, or at least some of them. I also had something that she didn't anymore: the element of surprise. I *knew* she was coming for me, but she would have no idea that I was coming for her. In fact, she would have zero reason to even suspect it. For all that she knew, Jackie was just studying in the library, not super-sleuthing mysterious disappearances.

There was hope here. I could actually do this. *I could do this.*

I jumped to my feet at the sudden spike in adrenaline and cried, "I can do this!" I instantly regretted the outburst as I felt the eyes of the other library occupants upon me. I mumbled an apology to the people closest to me before closing my laptop and carefully gathered my things as quietly as possible. This time I made sure to grab my car keys.

As I was walking toward the door, a college-aged guy leaned over from behind a bookshelf and whispered, "You can definitely do this." I gave him an embarrassed smile before stepping outside.

Jackie: thnx, jeremy. u always know just what to do.

V

IGNORING THE OVERWHELMING sense of deja vu, I started walking to the van, but paused to look around. There were cars everywhere. For all that I knew, that woman could be here, watching me right now. I studied the cars around me, searching for its red hue. Once I had convinced myself that I was not going to get jumped unexpectedly, I made a beeline for the Giordano family van. I didn't let myself catch my breath until I was safely seated inside the vehicle with the doors locked.

"Okay," I whispered to myself, breathing hard in response to the adrenaline pumping through my veins. "C'mon, Nessa, think. How do you get out of this one? How do you surprise an abductor?"

The element of surprise was the best thing I had going for me, something I could use to my advantage. If I found her first, I might be able to call the police and have her arrested before she took Jackie, or I could talk to her directly, somewhere safe, try to make her explain why she was doing this. Maybe this was where I could bring an end to all this.

But before I could think about turning her in, I needed to find her first. I couldn't see her from the parking spot, but that didn't mean she wasn't somewhere nearby. Tapping into the excited fear that gripped my core, I swiftly pulled out of the parking lot and onto the road. If I was going to figure out if she was following me or not, I needed to see if she was going to pull a similar stunt on Jackie that she did on Tony.

I drove for several minutes with nothing but the radio's static to accompany my thoughts. It felt strange not to have any music playing while I was on the road, but I wasn't in the mood. There was no way I'd be able to focus if I had The Who screaming in the background.

My plan was to drive past Jackie's house and around the general neighborhood to see if the woman showed her face again (or rather, her minivan). But when I stopped to let a group of children cross the street, I started feeling a pull. It was the same pull that overtook me while I was trying to text an excuse for Eliza not to go to the party. I was getting pushed to the back of Jackie's mind. There was something happening that I couldn't change, something vital to Jackie's past. Knowing that there was no point in resisting, I forced myself to swallow my fear and allowed her to take the wheel. She immediately began to brake and turn off onto her street.

There was something at her house, something that she needed to see.

As soon as she made the final turn onto the Giordanos' road, I could sense that something was different. I couldn't put my finger on it, but it made my heart race. Something big was at that house, something important.

Turns out, I was right. It was just sitting there, pulled

tight against the curb, looking as shiny and chic as ever: Tony's truck.

"Tony?" Jackie gasped, revving the engine and speeding toward the familiar vehicle. The sight of it made me stiffen at the back of Jackie's mind, knowing full well it was most likely not driven there by Jackie's twin. It was parked against the curb in front of their house but a few feet from the driveway, so Jackie had to drive past it in order to park the car. As she turned into the driveway, she slowed down to peer into the driver's side.

There was no one there. The front seat was empty.

After Jackie parked, I stepped to the front of Jackie's mind to take back control. I looked around cautiously. I listened. So quiet. Not even a dog or a bird. From what I could tell, there was no one nearby. Someone had been here recently, but I had sickening feeling it wasn't Tony.

I moved slowly toward the car, wary, like the engine would rev on at any second. Once I was close enough, I peered into the windows, cupping my hands around my eyes to block out excess light. The interior was exactly as I remembered it, complete with a crumpled receipt on the dashboard and an empty fast food bag scrunched in the cupholder. If I hadn't known better, I would've believed exactly what Jackie thought now: Tony was home. But I knew better.

Someone had obviously driven the truck here. But where were they now?

Just as the thought crossed my mind, I heard gravel crunch behind me. I whirled away from the car, hairs standing erect on the back of my neck. The unmistakable feeling of being watched swept over me, and I felt my stomach churn.

"Tony?" Jackie called, standing on her toes to fully look

around. "Is that you?" Jackie tried to keep her voice even, but her jangled nerves cracked the words.

We stood there in the tense silence, waiting for what seemed like hours to both Jackie and me.

Just when I was beginning to think I had officially gone insane and there was no one there, a slight figure emerged from the narrow entryway. She wore faded jeans and a well-worn blouse. Her steps were small but steady as she walked toward me. The woman wore the years well, and I recognized her almost immediately. I quickly halted the question Jackie had poised on the tip of her tongue and instead asked my own: "Are you Nancy Harding?"

The woman paused mid-stride. Her lips curled upward into smile. "Yes." Her voice was smooth and crisp with no trace of an accent.

I nodded, a sense of relief washing over me. At last, I knew who was behind all this. Now came the real question. "Why are you following me?" Even though I didn't continue the second part of the question, I could feel it hanging between us: *Why are you following me… and where's Tony and Eliza?*

Harding cocked her head to the side. She seemed genuinely confused. "I'm not following you," she replied. "I'm helping you search for your brother."

I blinked at her. That wasn't the response I was expecting. Was she being serious? As I began to form a reply, she began stepping toward me. I was too frazzled to stop Jackie from stepping forward. "Have you seen him?" she asked, desperation soaking through her words.

Harding nodded, continuing to walk toward me. I began stepping back. For some reason I couldn't explain, I didn't want her to come any closer. "Yes, I just saw him park his truck. But I don't know where he went."

My eyes flitted around the street. We were alone. She didn't seem like much of a threat right now, but I had a feeling that could change in an instant. My mind raced, attempting to think of what to do next. I had Harding right in front of me. Why was I freezing now?

There were only a few steps between us. Her mouth remained in a small tight-lipped smile, but something about her eyes unnerved me. Suddenly, I realized why I was so tense.

"Wait!" I blurted, and she paused. My heart sunk in my chest as the words slipped past my lips. "How did you know my brother's missing?"

The Giordanos never told anyone Tony was missing. There was no way she could know, unless…

She froze. "I heard you call his name," she answered smoothly, but I saw the corner of her mouth twitch.

"How did you know my brother's name is Tony?"

There was a moment of silence. Then, without warning, a car alarm started blaring. It wasn't until I saw the flashing hazard lights and determined the sound was coming from Tony's car that I realized my mistake. By the time I turned back, Harding was inches away, reaching toward my neck with what looked like a black cartridge. I heard the sharp sizzle of electricity and the connection snapped into place: *Taser.*

In an instant, I threw my left arm up to force her hand away. She stumbled, off-balance, and I lifted my right elbow to bring it down squarely on her collarbone. The sharp contact sent a shooting pain up my arm. Harding grunted, falling to her knees in front of me with Tony's keys clutched in one hand and the Taser in the other.

For a single moment, I reveled in the small victory. Damn, those self-defense moves really worked. But the one second I let my guard down was one second too many. A hand wrapped itself around my ankle, and suddenly, the ground was racing toward me. My back hit the concrete, knocking the wind out of me. Suddenly, Harding was on top of me, her knees pressing down on my chest. I couldn't breathe, my lungs unable to expand under the pressure. My wide eyes met Harding's. She was still grinning.

"Don't worry," she whispered, angling the Taser above me. Strings of blue light crackled from one end. "I know you're confused. But everything will make sense soon."

There was a pinch on my neck, followed by a white-hot burn that spread from limb to limb.

And then there was darkness.

VI

I SHOT UP in bed, frantically rubbing my arms. It was like the echo of electricity still coursed through my veins, reminding me of the horror in which I fell asleep. My heartbeat was frantic and uneven in my chest, my breathing short and gasping. I wiped at my eyes, feeling the moisture dampening the lashes.

Jackie was attacked. That woman, Nancy Harding, used a freaking *Taser* against her. I wasn't prepared for a Taser. I wasn't prepared for any of this. I thought I'd be safe there, out in the open. But like everything else I assumed about this mess, I was wrong.

As moment by moment slipped by, eventually, my pulse slowed and the room came into focus. Once I realized where I was, I felt my hands begin to shake. "Oh no." I breathed. "Oh no no no no…"

I was in *my* bedroom. Not Eliza's or Tony's or Jackie's. *Mine*. I held my hands in front of me, studying them, then pulled a lock of hair in front of my face. I was back in my own body. Whatever had just happened was over. There were no more memories to relive.

Now, it was my turn.

I spun around to face the wall, pulling my phone, cord and all, from the outlet. The home screen told me it was March 5. "March 5," I repeated, crunching the numbers silently. "That was only… a week and a half after Jackie was taken. And…" I thought back for a second before realizing, "Zero days since I left my body." Yesterday I talked to Mrs. Barrows about the "Missing Person" posters. Not a day had passed. I still had time to stop this. I now had a name, times, dates, victims—everything I needed to convict Harding. There was no way to explain how I had this information, but if I could make one person believe, just *one* person, it would be enough to stop this.

It wasn't even seven o'clock. There was still time before the school bus came. I could run to Eliza's house, explain everything to Mrs. Barrows, and be back in time to make it to school. But if I was going to make it, I had to move quickly.

Adrenaline raced through my veins as I ripped off my pajamas and threw on the first set of matching clothes I could find. A pair of Keds caught my eye, and I shoved them onto my sockless feet as I half-tumbled down the stairs.

"Nessa?" I cringed when my mother's concerned voice echoed up the stairwell. "Are you all right?"

"Yeah!" I called back, praying she wouldn't follow me out the door. "I just need to run to the Barrows' real quick!"

"You're going to the Barrows' house?"

"Yeah, I'll be right back!"

"No, Nessa, stop!" I heard her striding toward me, and I swung open the front door. "You can't just leave—"

"Just give me ten minutes!"

Her shouted reply was cut off when the door slammed

shut behind me. She wouldn't understand. I needed to get there now. Who knew how much time I had before Harding came for me. I stepped onto the bottom step, preparing to sprint down the driveway.

I felt it before I saw it. While my one foot met the hard concrete, the other connected with something soft. I froze. My gaze fell to the sidewalk.

A small square blanket lay in the middle of the porch step, clean but worn. Slowly, I bent down to pick it up between my thumb and forefinger. I waited for a vision to appear like it had with the others, but there was nothing. There were no more memories to see. This was my life now. I was finished reliving someone else's.

The blanket confirmed my worst fear: Somehow I was a part of this too, along with Eliza and Jackie and Tony. The connection had been there all along. Through all the time I had spent in their minds, we were connected through Nancy Harding.

There was no time left. She was already here. And not only that—

I was next.

"Oh God..."

PART FOUR

Vanessa

I

WHEN I STEPPED back into the house, I barely registered the door closing behind me. I couldn't think, couldn't breathe. I could only stare at the baby blanket clenched between my fingers. My mind throbbed, two words beating in rhythm with my racing heart.

I'm next I'm next I'm next I'm —

"Vanessa?" My head shot up, gaze locking with my mother's. Her eyes were wide with anger and confusion. "What are you doing? You can't just run out of the house, you need to go to school."

I blinked, hearing her words but not processing them. No, I needed a plan, needed to know what to do next. Harding was coming for me, I needed to do *something*. I tried to force my brain to focus, to think. For the others, it had been so easy. But now that this was my life that was being played with, suddenly coming up with a plan on the fly wasn't so easy anymore.

"I-I can't..." I closed my eyes, fighting against the fear that threatened to overwhelm me. "I just—I need to think for a moment."

"Is there something wrong?" A pause, then, "You look pale. Are you feeling alright?"

"No. I mean, yes, I'm fine, I just…"

There was a hand on my shoulder. I slowly opened my eyes and lifted them to my mother. The confusion in her face had shifted to concern. I saw the question there behind her eyes: *What's wrong?*

I wanted to tell her. With all of my being, I wanted to tell her everything I had been through, everything I had seen. But I knew I couldn't. If I was standing in her shoes, listening to my story, there was no way I'd believe what I had to say.

What could I tell her? What proof could I give her that what I was saying wasn't complete fiction? There weren't any news articles written about Tony or proof that he had been abducted. I could always check online to see if the Giordanos had reported Jackie missing, but I doubted it. If Harding had covered her trail for Tony, she had probably done the same for Jackie. What about the flashbacks? Could I try to explain them? And the toys? That sounded crazy, but not as crazy as me living in another person's body, reliving their memories. But what good would that do? I still didn't know how the four of us were related to the children I saw in the visions. And my adoption theory had been proved wrong for Jackie and Tony, so unless someone else was adopted—

My eyes widened as it hit me. Adopted. The blanket I found confirmed that I was a part of this cycle, that I was next on Harding's list. Tony and Jackie hadn't been adopted. But what if…

What if…

"Mom," I began. "Please be honest with me." My mother looked at me, confused as I worked up the last bit of courage I had in me. I knew if I thought about it too long, the words would never transfer from my mind to my mouth. So I forced them out before my brain had time to convince me otherwise. "Am I adopted?"

When I saw the stunned look on her face, I thought I had made the same mistake I had with Mr. Giordano. But it slowly shifted to something else. Something that looked… *sad.*

"Well," she whispered, "it was only a matter of time."

Hold on…

"Wait." I stared at my mother. "Am I really?"

My mother looked at me a moment before replying, "Yes."

No, this wasn't supposed to be true. I was supposed to be wrong, like I was with Jackie. Maybe Jackie and Tony were adopted, but me*? There was no way, there had to be a mistake…*

"I was planning on sitting you down and having this talk with you at some point, but I guess now is as good a time as any." She shifted her weight from foot to foot, and I could tell she was measuring her words carefully. "It's true, you're adopted. But that doesn't change the fact that we chose you and that we love you. We're still a family."

I shook my head, saying, "No—I mean, understand, yes, we're a family. I want to know about my-my birth mother. What was her name?"

"Well, in all honesty, I don't know."

My face fell. "What do you mean, you don't know? Did you just pick me up off the street or something?"

"Of course not!" My mother took my hand, tugged me gently into the kitchen. We sat down together at the table. "We got you when you were about a year and a half. There had just been an incident, and you had to be transferred to a new family immediately. All I was told was your name was Vanessa and that your birth mother couldn't take care of you any longer. They wouldn't tell me anything else because it was classified."

I allowed myself to think through her words carefully, trying to make sense of it all. "So you don't know anything about my birth mother?"

"No," my mother replied with regret apparent in her eyes. "I wish I could tell you more, but they don't always give all the information to the adopting family. I'm sure if I contacted the agency now, they would tell you what you want to know. It's been so many years, I'd imagine we could access it now."

That would be too late. I swallowed, fighting against the tears brimming in my eyes. "Have you ever heard of someone named Nancy Harding?"

My mother tilted her head to one side, and I could tell she was thinking it over. "I don't think I know the name. Why are you asking?"

"It's nothing." Wiping angrily at the moisture clouding my gaze, I stood. I stepped past my mother and toward the staircase leading upstairs. "I'm sorry, I-I just need some time to process."

"Honey!" she called after me. I heard the desperation in her voice, the not knowing what to do or say. "I'll let you take it all in, but if you need to talk about anything else, just let me know."

My voice broke when I shouted back, "Okay!"

I could barely make it to my room before the dam broke and tears began to fall in full. My parents… weren't my real parents. We were family, but we weren't related by blood. That meant that I had another mother out there and another father.

And someone trying to abduct me.

I thought for sure if there was anyone who would be adopted, it would be Tony and Jackie but not… *me*. Not Vanessa, who had her life in perfect order. At least until her best friend went missing. Then everything went to shit.

Nancy Harding was responsible for all this. But why? Why

would she obsess over four children? Sure, maybe I was adopted, and *maybe* I had some long-lost relative in all this, but what about Jackie and Tony? They weren't adopted, and I'm pretty sure Eliza wasn't adopted either. And there was no way I could bring that up to Mrs. Barrows. So how did this all make sense? Why was I dragged into all this bullshit?

"Nothing makes sense!" The words burst from my lips, breaking in the air before falling lifeless to the floor. What had I been doing these last four days? I had moved from body to body, watching as person after person were ripped from their lives, and I was no closer to stopping her. I knew that she was coming after me next, but what was to say she would stop? What if she kept going and took more children? I'm assuming that the four children from the vision were somehow connected to the four of us, but there was always the chance I wrong. What if she didn't stop once she took me? What if she just kept going? Then all this would've been for nothing.

The blanket meant Harding was coming for me. There was nothing I could do to stop it. But she wasn't here yet. There was still time for me to do something to stop this. I needed to find where Harding was now. She had to be nearby if she left the blanket for me. Maybe, with a little more digging, I could uncover more before it was too late.

I blinked away the last of my tears. I couldn't waste any more time. There would be time to cry when this was all over. But for now, I needed to use whatever time I had left as best I could.

I ran to my bed, dragged my laptop from its case, and flipped it open. Spotify was still open from the last time I had used it, paused halfway through Billy Idol's "White Wedding, Pt. 1." I pressed play, head instantly moving to bop with the beat. With the pounding rhythm there to move my thoughts, I typed in

"Nancy Harding" and set the window to the last month. The search drew no results. I tried the last year, still no luck. The only thing I could find was the same police report I had found in the library, about the charges filed against her. It was as if Harding was involved in the incident on the highway, then disappeared for sixteen years. Until now.

Next, I searched Jackie's and Tony's names again to see if anything would come up. I wasn't completely surprised when I couldn't find a "Missing Person" report. I felt like I was a car with dull tires, wheels spinning round and round without moving a single inch.

As I lay in bed, I felt a sudden wave of exhaustion wash over me. I had been running on adrenaline for the last four days, and I didn't think the hours of sleep I got were rolling over from person to person whom I inhabited. Physically and emotionally, I was drained. My gaze fell to the bed beneath me, and my limbs felt leaden. I needed sleep. As soon as I considered the thought, I couldn't get it to leave my mind. If I didn't rest for a few minutes, I wouldn't be able to function. Besides, maybe when I woke up, I would have a fresh perspective and be able to figure out what was going on.

As soon as I closed my laptop and my head hit the pillow, an overpowering wave of exhaustion swept over me. My eyelids felt like two weights falling over my eyes. I wasn't strong enough to resist their pull, and I fell into a deep slumber.

III

WHEN NEXT I woke, I instantly knew that something was different. The first indication was the darkness that filtered through the window. It was dusk, turning to night.

"Oh crap," I murmured, sitting up on the heel of one hand and rubbing the sleep from my eyes. I could already tell I had slept way longer than I wanted to. "What time is it?" I found my phone under one of the covers and checked the time. "Four thirty-four?" I read in horror. The day was practically over. I must've been more exhausted than I thought. Even though I knew I needed the sleep, I couldn't believe how much of the day was already gone. The more I thought about it, the more I realized how stupid I had been. I was lucky that Harding didn't come and kidnap me in my sleep. I blinked, glanced around, and laughed shakily. Well, at least I was in the same body. It's the little things to be thankful for.

As wakefulness returned to my mind, I remembered just how much had changed since I woke up as Vanessa. The blanket I had found and then the whole adoption thing… I shook my head, already longing for the return of sleep's ignorant bliss. Much as I had hoped that I would wake up with some revelation to fix it all or some sudden realization where everything would click into place, neither had occurred while I slept. What I did wake up with was hunger.

And in the end, the hunger was what got me moving. As I swung my legs over the side of the bed, my eyes caught a note taped to my cell phone. I reached for it and instantly recognized the slanted cursive of my mother.

Nessa,

I'm sorry today didn't go as smoothly as I'd hoped. I really had been planning on finding a good time to tell you, but every time I thought I was ready, it never seemed to work out. The day we picked you up from the adoption center was the best day of my life. I know your father feels the same way. You are a part of this family now and forever, and you will always be our little girl. Nothing will ever change that.

I understand you've had a rough morning, so I let you sleep through the afternoon. I also called your school and told them that you were sick. I was planning on staying until you woke up, but I needed to go into work. I'm so sorry I'm not there for you right now. If you need anything, don't hesitate to call.

I love you, Vanessa.

Mom

P.S. I found some leftover chocolate-peanut butter ice cream in the freezer. It's all yours. :)

I couldn't help but smile at my mother's written words. She really was trying her best. I stood, running a hand through my hair to calm the frizz. I felt refreshed and renewed, even if I didn't have a plan laid before me. I made my way down the stairs. The house was abnormally quiet after the frenzied events from this morning. My eyes darted to the fridge in the kitchen, and I felt my stomach growl in anticipation. I swung the door open and felt the cool air kiss the bare skin of my hand. Spotting the pint from my mother's message, I grabbed it and shut the door. Before I sat down, I slid a spoon from the drawer and shoved it straight into the center of the carton. Sure, it wasn't the best meal, but I felt like I deserved it after the hell I had been through these last few days. It seemed surreal to sit there in the quiet, enjoying the swirl of peanut butter and chocolate. The situation was something strangely normal in the most abnormal of circumstances.

As I slowly ate and digested both the food and the situation at hand, I had the sudden, inexplicable feeling that something was wrong. I touched the front pocket of my jeans, feeling for a familiar weight. Yes, my phone was there. I glanced toward the fridge, wondering if I had forgotten to shut it, but no, that wasn't it either. My eyes moved to the window, searching for something in the waning light. Contrary to my seemingly inexplicable intuition, everything seemed fine. But that still couldn't explain the hairs standing up on the back of my neck or the shiver that raced down my spine. And just when I thought that I was imagining it, that there was nothing wrong after all—

The lights went out.

Not just the lights. All the power. Every electronic in the house went completely still. If I thought the house was quiet before, now it was deathly still.

I couldn't help but gasp, "Oh shit," before slamming my jaw shut. She knew that I was here. She knew I was alone.

This was it. She was coming for me.

As the adrenaline flooded my mind, the seconds slowed to minutes, which gave me time to think. After being in so many stressful situations over the past few days, I found my mind surprisingly calm. I visualized all the possible scenarios in seconds. Making a run for the front door wasn't an option. She would be looking for that, and I had already seen what she could do to someone out in the open. She was clever and creative, which meant I had to be even more so. I knew the layout of the house better than she did. If I could hide and call for help, I might be able to wait her out until help arrived.

But first, I needed something to protect myself. My eyes scanned the kitchen before stopping on the knife block. I crept on the balls of my feet to the counter, grabbing the largest knife we owned. It felt strange and unnatural in my hand. In the movies, the heroes had always looked so normal when they held it, like they were used to holding a potentially deadly weapon in their hand. I, on the other hand, had no experience with anything even remotely dangerous. I shifted the knife until I found a semi-comfortable angle, then held it at my side. The hilt shook slightly in my hand. Armed to the best of my ability, I crept as quickly as I could toward the stairs leading up to the second floor. As I did so, I removed my cell phone from my pocket and dialed three numbers. A deep even-toned voice answered after a single tone.

"911, what is your emergency?"

Doing my best to ignore my racing heart, I forced my words out slowly. "There's someone breaking into my house."

"Okay, ma'am, what is your location?"

As I listed my address, I stepped carefully in my bedroom and shut the door, careful to muffle the sound. I was sure my mother locked all the doors before she left me alone in the house. Harding would have to break the lock to get inside. That would give me at least a few minutes for the police to arrive. Hopefully, it would be enough.

"What's your name?"

"Vanessa."

"Okay, Vanessa. Where are you in your house?"

"I'm in my bedroom, upstairs. I don't know where she is, she's probably trying to break through the front door."

"'She'? Have you seen this person?"

I paused, realizing my mistake. I didn't have the time to explain all this. Once they caught her, they'd figure out the truth. "I don't know if it's a he or a she. I just mean that they might be at the front door."

"Okay, I understand. No matter what happens, I need you to stay on the line with me, okay?"

"I will," I breathed, voice so low the sentence barely made it past my lips. I had moved into my closet now, and for once, I was thankful for how messy I kept it. The laundry in the corner provided enough cover for me to hide. I picked up a pile of it before squatting down and covering myself with it. It actually did a decent job of concealing my figure. I was even able to use my foot to tug the door almost fully close. The way I was positioned, though, prohibited me from closing it all the way, so it left a few centimeters of space between the door and the wall. "I'm hiding in my closet. Please hurry."

"Someone has been dispatched to your location. They're on their way now."

I was preparing a reply when I heard the tinkling of glass

against tile. "Oh God, they're inside. I just heard a window smash. I think they're in the kitchen."

"Okay, Vanessa, I need you to stay calm and hold on until help arrives."

The phone was shaking in my grasp, and I shifted to clutch it with both hands. I thought the abduction would play out differently now that I was expecting it, but it was too soon. I wasn't ready for this. There was still so much to do. In the little time I had left, I knew I couldn't explain everything to the operator. I frantically searched my mind for someone I could tell. Who would believe me? A second later, a memory jumped to the forefront of my mind, and I nearly dropped my phone.

Someone already knew. They knew everything, and they didn't even realize it. I pulled the phone away from my face, pressed the home button. If I was going to pull this off, I had to be fast. Anything too long and Harding might see the light of the screen. Opening up the messages app, I sent ten words to Jeremy.

> **Vanessa:** the story is real. Nancy Harding is coming for me.

I sent up a prayer as I hit send. Jeremy was smart. He would be able to figure it out. I suddenly became aware that the operator was speaking again, and I pressed the phone back to my ear.

"Vanessa, can you hear me?"

"Yes."

"Do you hear anything right now?"

I paused to listen. At first, I couldn't make anything out

over my breathing, so I put up one hand to my mouth to stifle my exhalations. And that's when I realized.

I could *still* hear breathing. Someone was in the room, close enough that I could make out their every breath. The operator was saying my name, but I couldn't answer. Not when she was so close. I stayed as still as I could, willing every muscle in my body to tense and turn to stone. I squeezed my eyes shut as tight as I could, as if just by looking around I could give away my location.

There was silence for what seemed like hours.

And then the closet door swung open. I heard it, felt the subtle rush of new air. I willed myself to be still, prayed that she wouldn't see my hunched figure. And for a second, I thought it had worked.

Then the clothes were pulled from on top of me. My head shot up, wide eyes meeting hers.

"Hello, sweetie." Harding grinned at me. I could just make out the outline of her head, but her expression was veiled in darkness. My eyes fell to the Taser in her hand. "Mommy missed you so much."

I had no time to think, barely any time to react. I watched her swing down, Taser in hand. In that fraction of a second, I shoved my phone into my back pocket and held up my knife. But her aim was true, and I felt metal tongs connect with the side of my neck. Every muscle in my body tensed at once, and then everything went dark.

IV

ONE OF MY favorite scents has got to be the musky smell right after a rainfall. My AP Environmental Science teacher explained that the smell is actually pollen and organic particles kicked up by the fallen water, but the less-than-appealing description doesn't take away from how soothing the smell is. Even if the sidewalks are dry and the moisture has long since evaporated, if you smell that signature scent, your mind automatically says "rain."

When I opened my eyes to darkness, the scent that met my nose screamed "fear." It was a putrid, hot mixture of body odor, dust, and metal. No, not metal. Blood. The combination was so gut-wrenching that I started to gag but found I couldn't move my arms. Or my legs. I was sitting in a chair, restrained by something that felt like thick rope. I strained against it, trying to feel for any weakness in the fibers, but there were none. The chair itself didn't even creak, despite my best efforts. I opened my eyes as wide as they would go, desperate to find some light to make sense of my surroundings, to no avail. I couldn't make out a thing in the pitch-black, not even shadows. As I twisted my head around to try and see behind me, the muscles in my neck spasmed. I let out a cry, spinning back around and grinding my teeth as the pain faded.

"Damn it," I hissed as my head pounded. "That bitch." After the words passed my lips, I felt a shift in the air. Something moved off to my left. I turned my head, more slowly this time, to stare at where the sound was coming from. I squinted hard, but there was only darkness. I was preparing to speak when…

"Vanessa?"

The voice was quiet, unsure and worn, but I would have recognized it anywhere. "Eliza!" Even though I didn't speak very loud, my voice sounded like a hurricane compared to her hoarse whisper. "Eliza, are you okay?"

"I… I think so." I pinpointed her voice to somewhere off to my left. "I'm just… really hungry."

I breathed a sigh of relief. After all this time, my imagination had run rampant picturing all the things that could've happened to her. Alive, safe, and here, right in front of me. But we weren't out of the thick yet. I had so much to ask her, but I had no idea where to start. "Where are we?"

"We're in her freaking basement." This voice was different but still familiar. Resilient, yet tinged with fear.

"Is that you, Jackie?" I asked.

There was a pause. "Do I know you?"

The pieces were slowly coming together in my mind. "No," I answered softly. "I guess not. Is your brother down here too?"

A deeper masculine voice responded from directly in front of me. "How do you know our names? What's going on?" I could tell he was trying to not to lose it, and to be honest, I was trying hard not to too.

"I can't explain now, there's no time." I spoke toward one twin. "Jackie, do you remember anything strange happening before you went missing?" There was an awkward, tense pause, and I realized how little they knew. Before I asked them any questions, I needed to give a little background. "Okay, I'm sorry. Let me start over. My name is Vanessa Stockton. I'm Eliza's best friend from high school. I think I can figure out what's going on here, but I need your help. I need you to trust me and tell me what you know. Please." A moment passed with no response, so I repeated, "Do you remember anything weird that happened before you were abducted?"

A moment of silence passed, and I wasn't sure Jackie would answer me, then, "There was this weird toy I found on the windshield of my mom's car. I had ditched school that day. I don't remember why. And there was this pinwheel thing stuck in my car. I thought it was weird, but I didn't think much of it. I went to the library to study, and when I got back, Tony's car was in front of the house. I thought that meant he was home, but I guess that lady stole it 'cause she was the only one who was there. And then she jumped me."

Tony interjected, speaking slightly too fast, "I found a toy too! A red car. But the lady must've drugged me or something. One minute, I was eating cookies, and the next, I was tied up here."

"And Eliza," I added, "you found a teething ring, right?"

"Yes," she breathed, and I heard the question behind her response: *How do you know this?* But there was no time to explain.

"When you picked up those toys, did you see anything strange? Or hear anything?"

There was a pause before Jackie asked, "What do you mean? Like, did we see the woman?"

"No." I tried to hint at it without giving away the answer. "I mean, like an image or something. Did you see anything like that?"

Their confused silence gave me an answer, solidified by Jackie's reply. "Uh no. Should we have?"

I thought on that for a moment, piecing it together. They didn't have any recollection of me being inside their minds. They just remembered their lives going about normally and then getting abducted. It was as if I was just an observer, witnessing events but not altering them. And that fit my experiences perfectly. I was able to change small things, but for big events, I was pushed to the back of my host's mind. I wasn't allowed to change the future.

"No," I said finally. "I don't think you were supposed to."

"Vanessa?" Eliza's voice was so soft, so tired, that I wasn't sure I heard it at first. It frightened me to hear her this weak.

"What is it, Eliza?"

"How long have I been here?"

I swallowed, hearing the desperation in her words. "Five months," I answered softly.

She gasped. "Five… five months?"

"We never stopped looking for you." I emphasized what I said next with every fiber of my being. "We did everything we could. We were talking to the police every day, following every lead we got."

I heard her sniffle, forcing herself to breathe deeply. "This is all my fault," she whispered. "I should never have left the house. I didn't even want to go to that stupid party." Her voice broke again. I could barely make out her next words between sobs. "How could I let myself get that *wasted?* How could I let this happen?"

"There's no way you could've known—"

"But I never should have been there in the first place. If I had just stayed home—"

"Hey!" Jackie cut in, voice harsh and unyielding. "I'm sorry, but it's too late for that 'woe is me' crap. We're stuck here now. This girl sounds like she's got her shit together or at least more than we do. So let's listen to what she's saying and figure out what the hell to do next. Once we're out of here, you can cry all you want. Sound good?"

It took several long moments for Eliza to control her tears. Eventually, she was able to reply, "Oh—okay."

"Okay. What's your name, new girl? Vanessa, was it?" She was using snarkiness to cope. I wasn't in the mood for humor, but if it helped her, then I would go along with it.

"Yeah."

"You know this Harding lady?"

"Well… kinda."

"How crazy is she?"

"Um… what do you mean?"

"I mean, she keeps calling me 'Peyton.' She calls Tony by his name—well, by 'Anthony,' but close enough—but she keeps calling me 'Peyton.' And she calls Eliza 'Ellie.' At first, I thought it was a mistake and she was just really bad with names or something, but whenever I try to correct her, she gets really pissed."

Tony interjected, "Yeah! And she wants us to call her 'Mom.'"

I was silent for a moment, unsure of how to respond. The different names, calling her "Mom," bringing us all here together… everything was coming together, but I still wasn't sure what it all meant.

I opened my mouth to attempt to put my thoughts into words, but Eliza whispered before I could speak, "She kept talking about getting one more person, one more girl. She always talked about you, saying how you were the most important, the special one. I had no idea… I always thought it would just be another random girl, but… I can't believe it's you, Nessa."

My stomach churned. "Why did she say I was 'special'?"

"She told us we would understand everything once you arrived."

Just as Eliza finished that sentence, a door opened somewhere above and behind me. The metal hinges squealed against the wood, a sound that set my teeth on edge. There was a soft click, and a single light bulb above us flickered to life. My eyes scanned the surroundings, taking in every detail of where we were being held.

Jackie seemed to be right. We were in some kind of a basement. There were no windows, only shelves holding every type of canned food imaginable. The light shining from above cast strange patterns of light and dark, and in the dim light, the shelves seemed almost like great towering shadows themselves. All four of us were strapped into chairs, facing one another in a near perfect square.

When my eyes found the form of my best friend, my heart nearly stopped. She was hunched over in a folding chair, restrained the same way I was. From where I was sitting, I could see her right eye was bruised and swollen. A dried trail of blood leaked from one corner of her mouth. Eliza turned to look at me, her once shining hair matted around her face. Although we exchanged no words, everything she needed to say was conveyed in a glance.

Tony and Jackie also looked rough, though not nearly as bad as Eliza. They were covered in grime, dark bags hanging under their eyes. Tony had a cut on his chin, but it seemed to be healing. They looked toward each other, seeming unnaturally calm considering the circumstances. Although they were seated apart, I could feel the bond between them. They were relying on each other to remain sane. Poor Eliza had no one until I arrived.

Then moving as one, all three of them turned to look behind me.

Clunk, clunk, clunk. Soft footsteps thudded hollowly as they descended what I assumed were stairs. I strained in my bindings, craning my head to see who was behind me. Eliza's face grew more and more twisted in fear until she forced her head downward to look at her feet.

There was one final creak of wood, then a step onto the concrete floor. My heart threatened to leap out of my chest as the sound grew closer and closer, until the footsteps were directly behind me. I jumped when a calloused hand caressed the back of my head.

"Hello, Brooke," Nancy Harding whispered in my ear. "I missed you so much, baby. Welcome home."

V

"WHY ARE YOU doing this?" I tried to make my voice defiant and sure, but I knew my expression betrayed my fear.

Harding ignored my question, moving to stand in front of me. With the additional light, I could see her in full. The overhead lights accentuated the natural smile lines and wrinkles in her face. Her green eyes scanned the four of us, her expression showing emotions that confused me: pride and excitement. Excitement at seeing us together? In her hands, she held an obviously homemade cake. Clumpy frosting covered the surface unevenly, and shaky red letters spelled out *WELCOME HOME* across the top.

"Look, everyone!" she exclaimed proudly, raising the cake so we could see. "I made you a cake to welcome you home!" Upon seeing the expressions on our faces, she gave a jagged laugh. "Oh, I know you can't eat it now. But once we leave and we've settled into our new home, we can enjoy it together." Harding placed it down in the center of the room between us before standing and dusting off her hands.

"We're moving someplace else?" Eliza asked softly.

"Of course, honey," Harding answered with a smile. "You didn't believe I was going to raise you down here, did you? No, this is all temporary. Once I finished reuniting your sisters and brother, I needed to return to Mount Sterling to pick our Brooke up. And as soon as we're finished down here, we can head out to start our new life together."

My mind was caught on two words. Against my better judgment, I lifted my gaze to meet hers. "Sister?" I repeated. "I don't have a sister. Or a brother."

Again, Harding laughed. The lighthearted action was completely contradictory to the situation at hand, and it made the hairs of on the back of my neck stand up. "Why, of course you do, you silly goose." She motioned to Jackie and Eliza. "In fact, you have *two* sisters."

"We're not sisters," I replied slowly. "Eliza and I… we're just friends."

Harding's head suddenly twitched to one side, but the moment passed, and she continued, "No no no, you've got it all wrong. Friends come and go. But family… family lasts forever." Harding rose to her feet and stood in the middle of our chairs. "I promised you we'd be together again. And here we are. I want you to understand—you *need* to understand. Just remember, no interrupting. Let Mommy speak." She turned to each of us, testing if anyone would contradict. No one did. Eliza's eyes remained locked on the floor.

After a moment of tension between us, Harding stepped back, satisfied. "You're about to start a brand new chapter in your life. Don't be frightened. You will soon see clearly that this is the way we were meant to be." She straightened her back and clapped her hands like an excited child. "We're going to be one big family!"

"Family?" Jackie narrowed her eyes. "What do you mean, family?"

Harding spun to face Jackie. Her eyes flashed, and Jackie instantly straightened. But Harding simply smiled. "I said no interrupting, Peyton." There was a pause, and then Jackie nodded slowly. Her eyes were glassy and wide with fear. Seemingly satisfied, Harding turned to face the rest of the group and continued, "Now, for Ellie, Peyton, and Anthony, you have been chosen to take on a special role, perhaps the most important role you will ever play. You will be three of the children in our family." The three exchanged looks, trying to piece this together. But I realized what she was going to say just as the words left her mouth. "Although none of you were originally cast in these roles, I know you will play the parts spectacularly. I've hand-selected you for a reason." Harding turned to look at me, grin still stretching across the tight skin of her face. "And you, Brooke. You were the one that took me so long to track down. Ever since I lost you on that highway, they tried to hide you from me. But I found you. A mother's love will always prevail."

My mind flashed back again to the car, the children inside. The screams. "I was in that car?" I whispered.

"Yes!" Harding threw her hands in the air, triumphant. She grinned from ear to ear, the relief evident in her voice. "Yes, that's right. You remember."

But… how? All the children died, except—

The baby. There was a baby with dark hair strapped into a car seat. She was too young to play the game, and she never took off her seat belt. She was the same child that took the teething ring from the toddler. And… that was *me.*

"I… I survived?" I breathed.

For the first time, I saw true anguish flit across Harding's face. "You were the only one." Her hands wringing themselves in front of her, she began pacing and continued, "Those damn cops wanted to take you all *away from me.* They said I was 'unfit to be a mother.' How dare they call me 'unfit'? Only a mother knows how to care for her children. And as soon as I heard they were going to take you away, I escaped with all of you. But they tracked me down, they wouldn't let me. They... they..." Her voice trailed away as tears choked her words.

It clicked. "They blew out the tires. Caused the car to crash."

Harding spun to face me, eyes shining with grief and pain. "They *killed* my babies. You, Brooke. You were the *only one who survived.* Tucked away in your little car seat."

As I struggled to wrap my brain around this, there was one thing I couldn't move past, my brain simply couldn't accept. I had to know the truth. "You're... you're my birth mother?"

Harding nodded, the smile on her face now one of sadness. "Yes, honey. Those other people you lived with—they aren't your real family." She motioned about the room. "*This* is your real family now. The family you always should've had. Before they took it all away from me." Her voice turned sad, almost regretful. "After the accident, you were all I had left, Brooke. And even *you* they took away from me. They sent me away to an institution to try to *fix* me. Those were the worst years of my life. But, Brooke..." Something deep inside me responded to the name, and I looked up. I watched a tear trickle down her face, and when she spoke, her voice was tight with emotion. "Thinking of you was the only thing that kept me going. And while I was there, I made plans. Plans to give you the life you always deserved. With us, your true family."

I realized what she was saying, and I barely registered the words as they passed my lips. "So you kidnapped Eliza, Jackie, and Tony to fill the empty places where Ellie, Peyton, and Anthony had been."

Harding nodded, rattling off the details as if she were bragging to a fellow parent about her children. And in her own mind, I guess she was. "Eliza was just about the right age for Ellie, and you and she practically acted like sisters anyway. I was just making it a reality. I ended up nabbing her after that little party she had. Then I found Tony, who shared the same name as my Anthony *and* had a twin sister. I knew that there could be no one else. It was perfect! The two of you were *meant* to be mine."

She turned to look at each of us, the grief in her words hardening to something darker. "You have to understand, I never wanted to hurt any of you, but I wanted to—*needed* to—have my family back. And the only way to do that was to rebuild it one person at a time. I think you'll come to find that you'll lead better lives this way. Your lives have purpose now. I will be your Mommy, provide everything you need. You'll never have to worry again."

There was a slight pause until Jackie cleared her throat. Her cockiness seemed to have mostly dissipated, and what remained was dark and calculating. Her voice remained steady, though her eyes were wide in fear. "Were you the one who left the pinwheel in my car?"

"Yes. When you were little, that was your favorite thing to play with. I left each of you a toy, somewhere you could find it. It was my way of telling you 'Mommy's coming.'"

As Harding continued to rattle on, I tuned her out, closing my eyes and clearing my mind. It was hard to concentrate when I could still hear her talking about how she hunted each of us down, but I had no other choice. I had to think of a plan. There wasn't much time. Harding said that once we were done here, she was going to move us somewhere else. Once we moved, it would get harder for law enforcement to find us. As long as we stayed here, there was a greater chance someone would connect the dots and possibly track down our location. There were no windows in this basement, no way I could visibly contact the outside world. I needed to send out our location, somehow, before we left. But what could I use? I didn't see any way to do this. I shifted in my chair, trying to get more comfortable.

And that's when I felt it. My cheeks flushed with excitement. My cell phone. She had somehow forgotten to take it out of my pocket. Eliza saw my eyes widen in shock and realization but turned away, pretending she hadn't. I forced my face back to a neutral expression, heart pounding wildly in my chest. Holy crap! Suddenly, I had a real chance here.

There had to be a way I could contact someone. I couldn't pull the phone all the way out to dial 911. Harding would see it and take it for sure. There had to be something I could do that was silent, that would let me contact emergency services—

Emergency. With the new models of the smartphone, they had a setting built in that let you contact the police by just pressing a few buttons. You didn't even have to unlock the cell phone. I closed my eyes, thinking back, trying to remember which buttons to press. Finally, the memory clicked into place. It was the lock screen button. I had to press it five times. Then my location would instantly be sent to the police. This might just work.

After sneaking a look at Harding to make sure she wasn't looking my way, I arched my back and held my breath. When I strained as far as I could, the tips of my fingers just brushed the top of the phone. I quickly put my arm down when Harding turned to look at me, and I nodded along to whatever she was saying. After what seemed like an eternity, she finally faced Tony again. I stretched back one last time, letting out a quiet huff of relief when I felt my phone gripped in both hands behind me. Making my movements as subtle as possible, I found the lock-screen button with my thumb and clicked it, counting in my head.

One, two, three, four, five.

My phone buzzed once in confirmation. I forced back the smile that threatened to light my face and reveal my secret. It was done. But I still had the phone behind me. I needed to get it back into my pocket before she noticed. I tried to tuck it into my back pocket, but I couldn't angle it right. After several seconds of struggling, I realized I couldn't do it. The only other option I had was to press it against the back of the chair and pray that Harding didn't notice it. I didn't have any other choice. I looked up and saw Eliza staring at me. Her eyes flicked to the object clutched behind my back, then up to my face. I gave her the subtlest of nods. A flicker of a smile passed over her face, but she quickly turned again to face forward.

Now, all I had to do was wait. I had no idea where we were or how long it would take the police to get here. Or if the button thing even worked. So at the moment, I needed to draw this out as much as possible, waste as much time as I could. It was a messy, shaking plan at best, but at least it was a plan. I had hope that all of us could get out of here alive, and that was all I needed. Luckily, Harding was still talking in her overly happy voice, rambling on with story after story about those damn toys.

Once there was a lull in her speech, I cleared my throat loudly to attract everyone's attention. "I have a question," I said slowly, deliberately. "Could you tell me about what I was like as a baby?"

"Yes, honey, of course." Harding smiled at me, relieved at my interest. The stress seemed to fade as her words shifted to a softer, more loving tone. "I would *love* to tell you. You were such a perfect baby..."

"And then," Jackie added, glancing to me for confirmation. I tilted my head in the subtlest of nods. "I'd like to hear more about our old house." I dipped my head to her in a subtle nod. Yes, this was what we needed. Keep her talking.

"Of course!" Harding bubbled. "Yes, whatever you'd like, I'll tell you anything!"

So began a disjointed, slanted retelling of my childhood. Her focus shifted quickly between talking to one of us, talking to herself, then seemingly talking to no one. Sometimes her train of thought would seem to lead somewhere, then completely derail itself and move to something else. Although Harding kept her tone lighthearted, there was a palpable tension in the air that the rest of us couldn't ignore.

Because she seemed so unstable, we tried to steer clear of anything that might upset her. It was hard to tell if she was on the verge of a breakdown, and we didn't want her to accidently go unhinged.

But I knew we couldn't distract her forever, and eventually, someone slipped up.

VI

AS THE MINUTES passed, I could feel the tension build in the air. The others didn't know what I knew, so they didn't know what we were trying to stall for. And even though I *did* know what was hopefully coming, it didn't make the wait any easier. The questions buzzed in my mind, making it difficult to focus on the conversation happening in front of me: *Where were the police? Were they even coming? What if the emergency call didn't work? What if we were waiting for something that would never arrive?* I tried to force them away, but each second that passed made them that much louder in my mind.

When an uncomfortable silence filled the room for the third time, I knew I couldn't ignore it any longer. "So," I began slowly, trying to keep my tone casual. "Were you a stay-at-home mom?" As soon as the words passed my lips and Harding's expression hardened, I realized the weight of what I had just said. I was alluding to another member of the family, one that she hadn't brought up. I had been trying to avoid the subject, but it seemed I had just accidently walked right into it.

Harding's eyes narrowed, her lips pursed. "Your father was

useless," she growled, more than a little animalistic. "I had to do *all* the work myself. He left me long ago, when I got pregnant with you. He was evil and selfish, leaving me alone with three kids and another baby on the way. He didn't care about you the way I do. We didn't need him then." She paused to smile at the group of us, but this smile was different from the loving one she gave us minutes prior. This one was jagged and sharp. "And we don't need him now." Catching the look on my face, she stepped toward me. "Oh, don't be sad, Brooke. You would've hated him anyway."

The frightened expression on my face that Harding had thought was about my lost father was actually about the secret I clutched behind my back. As Harding moved closer and closer to me, the phone became increasingly slippery with sweat and difficult to grasp. My hand was beginning to cramp, and Harding was still approaching me. Any second now, she was going to see it. I needed to try to get it back in my pocket. Trying to look like I was stretching, I pushed my shoulders back, maneuvering my hand so it was aimed at my back pocket, but my fingers fumbled—

And the phone slipped out of my hand.

The clatter that followed echoed through the room and stole every one of our breaths. Harding froze. Heavy silence pressed in on all sides. No one breathed. Harding moved first. She took another step toward me. Her eyes trailed down behind my chair. "What was that?" she whispered. Her eyes bored into mine, daring me to respond. I had nothing to say, and she knew it. Striding around me, I felt her lean on the back of my chair as she reached down. "Brooke, darling…" She walked to stand in front of me, staring in horror at the screen. "Emergency services?" Her mouth opened, one hand moving to cover it in shock. *"Why would you do that?"* The shock turned to anger, and the eyes that stared at me flashed dangerously. "why would you do that?"

"I'm sorry." I could barely breathe, my lungs forgetting how to take in air. "It-it was an accident."

"Don't lie to me!" Harding screamed, blood rushing to her face. She threw the phone across the room, and I heard glass break when it collided with the concrete wall. "Do you know what you've done? How could you turn against me, Brooke? We're a family!"

I shook my head, tears streaming down my cheeks. *Had I just killed us all?*

Harding paused mid-stride, reaching one hand up to tug at her hair. "No," she muttered to herself. "We *are* going to be a family. I won't let them take that away, not again. We need to get them out of here. Now." Harding strode toward one of the shelves. She swept her hands across the table, scattering a box of screws across the concrete floor as she searched for something. Then she paused. I watched her choose a worn cloth and a bottle of clear liquid. She doused the rag, gripping it in her left hand before moving to another shelf. The clinking of metal seemed magnified in the empty silence. She extracted something from one of the shelves before moving back toward us. There was a collective intake of breath when the edge of the kitchen knife caught the light. In her left hand, she held an old rag, damp with something I couldn't make out in the dull light.

"It's time for all of you to go back to sleep. When you wake up, you'll be safe." She turned to Jackie, smiling at her. "You first, Peyton."

Jackie shook her head fiercely as Harding stepped toward her, but no words left her mouth. I could read it in her eyes. She was scared for her life.

Harding raised the knife. "Now, don't make me use this, Peyton. We don't have time to waste."

Jackie closed her mouth. All humor and courage gone from her eyes, she stared at the blade with pure terror.

Tony strained against the chair, heaving with exertion. His gaze threatened to murder Harding where she stood. *"Get the fuck away from my sister!"*

Harding lifted her left hand slowly, knife still raised toward the girl. Jackie didn't move, eyes glued to the weapon. She strained away from the rag, but Harding pressed it to her lips. A second later, her head sagged down into her chest.

"*Jackie!*" Tony screamed, face contorted with sobs. "*Jackie, wake up!*"

"Shut up, Anthony!" Harding growled. Moving toward the boy, she knelt in front of him. He barely had time to react before the chloroform filled his nose and his eyes closed.

"Please," I begged as she faced Eliza. "You don't have to do this." But Harding didn't stop. As she stepped toward Eliza, my mind spun. Where were the police? What could I do? I needed to do something, make a distraction, *something*. Mind spinning, I blurted, "Don't take them—just take me. Brooke. I promise I'll never try to escape again. I'll-I'll be happy with you forever, just like you want. We can be happy, just the two of us. Just please, *please* don't take them."

The fight had completely drained from Eliza. She didn't resist when Harding pressed the cloth to her face. Her head lolled to the side, eyes rolling back in her head. When Harding looked at me, her green eyes were dark.

"No," I whispered hoarsely. "Please, stop…"

Harding stepped toward me, shaking her head. "I have spent the last ten years of my life missing you, Brooke. Missing your first words, your first step. Those are memories that *they* took away from me that I can never get back. But I can make up for it. I *will* make up for it. I swear on my life you will have the family you deserve. The *whole* family you deserve."

If she took us away, they wouldn't be able to find us. We would be gone forever. With Harding less than a yard away from where I sat, I sent up one last desperate prayer.

You don't want it to end like this. You can't have brought me all the way here to be taken. You can't *let us be taken. Please,* don't let us be taken.

She was less than a foot away, reaching toward me with the rag. And in that fraction of a second, I suddenly remembered who was standing in front of me. Two word bubbled up from deep within me, demanding to be released, and I screamed them at the top of my lungs.

"Mom, stop!"

Harding froze. Looked at me. Her eyes shined with sorrow, pain—and hope.

For a moment, everything was still.

And then all hell broke loose.

From behind me, I heard an ear-shattering crash and footsteps pounding down the stairs. "Police!" a man called. "Drop the weapon and put your hands behind your head!"

Harding's eyes shot up, hope vanishing, her face a mask of fury. She shoved past me toward the person, letting out an inhuman scream that I could feel in my very bones. Her push sent my chair toppling over, with me still strapped into it. With no way to protect myself, I watched the ground rush toward me.

I felt my head crack against the concrete. Everything went dark.

VII

MY EYES BLINKED open, burning slightly from a white light. Looking down, I was surprised to find myself standing. I was on a highway, a yellow-painted line directly beneath my feet. As everything came rushing back, I pressed a hand to the side of my head that had hit the ground, expecting to feel some kind of pain from where it hit the floor. But no, there was nothing.

Was I dead? Maybe, but… maybe not. Something didn't feel right.

The whole place was shrouded in a thick white mist, making it difficult to see in front of me. Craning my head left and right, I noticed another thing that struck me as odd. The road was completely empty, not a car in sight. Maybe this was another vision? A memory? As my gaze ran over my surroundings, I realized that I knew this place. I knew this road, and I knew that highway sign.

That's when I saw them.

The mist seemed to part around them, revealing their shapes to me slowly. I didn't jolt, didn't jump. Even though I knew I should've been scared to see them, I wasn't. The three children stood on the side of the road, two girls and a boy. The blond girl held a red pinwheel. The dark-haired girl and boy held hands. They looked at me with wide, reflective eyes.

Ellie, Peyton, and Anthony—they looked identical to how I had seen them in the visions. Why was I seeing them again? Weren't we all safe? Hadn't we been rescued?

Deep down, I knew I was alive. But I was still missing something.

As I looked upon their three small fragile figures, I felt that tickle in the back of my mind. I had seen them before but not just in the vision. And that's when I remembered. I remembered it all.

When I was in Eliza's mind, I had seen three children playing outside when Trevor drove to the party. The first time I went to the library as Tony, there was a mother reading to her three children. When I was driving home as Jackie, I had stopped at a street light to let three children cross the street.

Three children: Ellie, Anthony, and Peyton. They were always with me, all three of them. I had seen them again and again but never made the connection. Until now.

"It was you," I whispered to my brother and sisters. "It was you the whole time. The visions, the memories... you let me see it all. You knew what was going to happen, and you tried to warn me." They didn't say anything, didn't even blink, but the air between us was filled with resolution. My mind flashed back to all those times I had seen the children. Always three. "And you were there the whole time. I hadn't even known it, but you were with me." A smile crept across my face, a tear trailed down my cheek. "You never left me. "

Ellie looked toward her siblings, a questioning look on

her face. When Anthony nodded, she stepped forward, away from the line. She approached me slowly, and as she did, I saw her skin had an almost fuzzy sheen to it, like it wasn't completely solid.

It wasn't until she was directly in front of me that I realized she held something in her hands: a stuffed bear. Ellie stopped in front of me, beaming blue eyes meeting mine. She held the bear toward me, smiling.

I sniffed, wiping my eyes. "Thank you, Ellie." I started to reach out, then paused. Looking to my sister, I asked, "Will I ever see you again?" When she smiled again, it was sadder, more solemn. She nodded, and I understood. We would see each other again, just not in this life. I nodded in return then looked toward Anthony and Peyton. There was one thing I needed to say to them, something I never had the chance to say.

"I love you," I whispered.

Ellie grinned wider, showing tiny white teeth. She bit her lip, lifting the bear higher. I knew it was time for me to go. Taking one last long look at my siblings, I reached out to take the toy.

And then there was darkness.

Epilogue

IT'S A STRANGE thing to have something you never knew you were missing in your life be suddenly given to you. It's an even stranger thing to have that same something taken back as suddenly as it was given.

I met my birth mother the same day she was killed, shot by the police who saved us. That single fact will haunt me for the rest of my life. It's not something that I can forget or therapy can fix. It's just something that's a part of me now, something I have no choice but to live with.

Even though I knew now that the woman I thought of as Mom for most of my life biologically didn't fit the title, it didn't matter. Sometimes you're not born into your true family. Sometimes your true family ends up finding you somewhere along the way.

I looked toward my mom, taking in her frizzy brown hair and tired but loving eyes. She glanced away from the road to throw me a look, feeling my gaze on her. "What?" she asked.

"Nothing," I replied smoothly, turning to face the road again.

My mother paused before looking back at the road. After the harrowing experience of being abducted and held captive, she hadn't really pushed me to say anything I hadn't wanted to. She knew I was still working through it all. Besides, although I don't remember much after I was knocked out, apparently, I had been the one to save everyone. Jeremy had thought my text about Nancy Harding was pretty weird, and when I didn't respond to his follow-up text, he let my mom know about it. By then, the police were already at our house, alerted by the frantic 911 call I made from the closet. All they needed was a lead, which I gave to them using the emergency function on my phone. They surrounded the house, which Harding had rented under a fake name, and were able to save all of us. Tony and Jackie had been transported home for evaluation, and Eliza remained in the local hospital for some time, recovering from malnourishment. Eliza told me that Trevor had visited her there and was practically in tears, apologizing again and again for making her go the party at Emma's. As I knew she would, Eliza forgave him. It's just not her nature to hold grudges. I saw firsthand that Trevor could be overbearing at times, but I could tell he did care about her deeply.

Harding was gunned down after attempting to assault a police officer with the knife she was wielding. She later died in the ICU. I was one of the only people who attended her funeral. As I stared at the grave site of this woman, the woman who had destroyed my life when she took Eliza and destroyed the Giordanos' when she took their children, I knew I should hate this woman, should despise her for everything that she did, everything that she took.

But I found that I couldn't. I tried to hate her, to burn

with rage I knew I should feel, but I didn't. She didn't do any of it maliciously. She didn't think what she had been trying to do was selfish at all. In her mind, it had all made sense: She was just taking back what was hers. Even after everything she had done, I found I couldn't hate her. I couldn't say that I would be missing her, but there was a part of me that thought if maybe she had gotten the help she needed, things might've been different. But it was too late for that now.

Although when I said my final goodbyes to my birth mother I was alone in the graveyard, I had a feeling there were three others at the gravesite with me. And that was all the company I needed.

My mother glanced at the radio station the car was set to. "Is this song okay, Nessa?"

It took me a second to identify the title entering through the speakers, but it eventually came to me. "Turn the Page," Bob Seger & The Silver Bullet Band. "Yes," I answered. It seemed to fit the situation well.

Nodding at my response, she narrowed her eyes out the windshield. "Do you know if we're close? We've been driving on this road for quite a while."

"We're close." Blurs of trees and signs passed alongside us, but there was only one sign I was looking for. Another few seconds passed before I spotted it. "Start slowing down. It's right up ahead." As the car began to slow, I reached toward the back seat, picking up a large bulky bag and placing it on my lap. "Here," I said. Once we had completely stopped, I removed my seat belt and stepped out.

The site was small, barely noticeable on the side of the highway. I had driven past it several times without even knowing it existed. Now, however, I paid careful attention to the wilted flowers and weather-worn crosses. From my bag, I withdrew three metal crosses and propped them up amid the other gifts. Each of them was inscribed with a name. *Ellie. Anthony. Peyton.*

I knelt before the crosses, eyes running over the names. My mother stood behind me, placing a hand on my shoulder. Nothing needed to be said. I closed my eyes, feeling the flower stems beneath my knees and the tangible presence of three others. I smiled.

We were a family again.

Acknowledgments

Well, that's another one in the bag! A debut always has a certain magic to it, but I found that this novel took on a life of its own as I continued pursuing it. And that's all thanks to the following people:

Mama and Padre, I am forever grateful for all the help you've provided me. From writing tips to emotional support, I would not be where I am today without you. Yet again, the parental relationships in this book were based in no way on my own experiences. I'm not sure where the inspirations for creating these unstable parental units come from, but it's definitely not from home. Thank you a million times over!

As for my little bros, thanks for all the times I asked you to turn down the television when I was working or pause your video games when I was filming. I know I can be annoying at times, but your compassion and understanding does not go unnoticed. Never stop being crazy!

Friends who have stuck with me since the beginning: your support and ability to talk me off the deep end is invaluable.

Special thanks to Emma, Meghan, Molly, Jane, and Sneha. Love you, ladies!

To my lovely beta readers: you were all absolutely brilliant! I cannot thank you enough for each and every second you've spent working with me on *Missing Her*. I'm forever grateful for the time, effort, and hard work you sacrificed for my work. I will gladly help you edit any college term papers you need!

I've had the privilege to meet some amazing fellow writers over the past few months. These talented individuals have been so supportive, and this book might not have happened without them. This goes out to Zachary James, Mandi Lynn, Kristen Martin, and countless others. I'm honored to consider myself part of the Writing Community.

A huge thanks is also due to all my online followers and subscribers! Thank you for your interest and passion for my work. I feel truly grateful for all the inspiration I've received, and I'm not sure where I would be without all of you. Just keep writing!

To all the people who have inspired me in ways big and small, you're a part of this book as well. Some of your influences are more obvious than others. Some of you may not even realize that I'm writing about you. Either way, you are a part of *Missing Her*.

I thank God for helping me utilize my gift in this creation and St. Francis de Sales for the prominent role he's played in my life. Veritas!

Finally, I thank you. If you're reading this book, you've inspired me to bring Vanessa, Eliza, Tony, Jackie, and all the others onto paper. Storyteller, in my opinion, is one of the greatest titles one can hold. But the stories cannot be told if there is no one to listen.

About The Author

J. L. Willow voraciously read everything she could get her hands on as a child and continues to this day. She was inspired by the way words on a page could capture the imagination, beginning her journey as a writer at just six years old. When she's not holding a pencil or a book, she can be found belting her favorite musicals or studying to become a mechanical engineer. Days off are spent relaxing with her family in New Jersey. Her debut novel *The Scavenger* was published in November 2017.

Vanessa's Playlist

"Back in Business" — AC/DC
"Wish You Were Here" — Pink Floyd
"Karma Chameleon" — Culture Club
"T. N. T." — AC/DC
"Turn the Page" — Bob Seger
"What Is and What Should Never Be" — Led Zeppelin
"Barracuda" — Heart

CPSIA information can be obtained
at www.ICGtesting.com
Printed in the USA
LVHW031309010421
683210LV00009B/473

9 780999 252628